# TARA'S GOLD

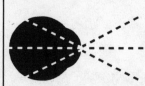

This Large Print Book carries the
Seal of Approval of N.A.V.H.

WILD PRAIRIE ROSES, BOOK TWO

# TARA'S GOLD

## LISA HARRIS

**THORNDIKE PRESS**
*A part of Gale, Cengage Learning*

GALE
CENGAGE Learning™

Detroit • New York • San Francisco • New Haven, Conn • Waterville, Maine • London

**LIBRARY OF CONGRESS CATALOGING-IN-PUBLICATION DATA**

Harris, Lisa, 1969–
    Tara's gold / by Lisa Harris. — Large print ed.
        p. cm. — (Wild prairie roses ; bk. 2) (Thorndike Press large print Christian romance)
    Originally published: Uhrichsville, OH : Barbour, 2007.
    ISBN-13: 978-1-4104-2445-7 (alk. paper)
    ISBN-10: 1-4104-2445-6 (alk. paper)
    1. Large type books. I. Title.
PS3608.A78315T37 2010
813'.6—dc22                                        2009049137

Published in 2010 by arrangement with Barbour Publishing, Inc.

Printed in the United States of America
1 2 3 4 5 6 7 14 13 12 11 10

To my aunt Janelle, who's always been an example to me on how to serve God with one's whole heart.

# ONE

*July 1870*
*Tara Young stuck her hand into the satin lining of her fringed jacket. The thin paper crinkled between her fingers, assuring her of its presence. All she had to do was carry the message into the mercantile and pass it to the young clerk who worked there. A simple task considering her last assignment. Stopping in front of the sheriff's office, Tara measured the distance between her and the front door of the store. Ten steps, maybe eleven. A quick look down the boardwalk, which ran parallel to the town's whitewashed storefronts, confirmed her assessment that no one was paying attention to her.*

*And why should they? There was no reason for anyone to sense anything out of the ordinary with her presence in the busy passageway. She looked like any other fashionable young woman out for a day of shopping for ribbons or perhaps a peek at the latest*

7

*dress fabric that had just arrived from the East. There was no cause to suspect her of carrying confidential information on the war. No grounds for anyone to guess she was a spy for her country.*

*A man stepped in front of her, his boots clanking on the wooden flooring. The afternoon sun caught the shiny ivory handle of a gun beneath his black overcoat. Tara swallowed hard. The moment of truth had arrived. And this time, she was ready.*

Tara's head smacked against the back wall of the stagecoach, jarring her from her slumber. She sucked in a deep breath of air and held herself upright, hoping the other five occupants of the horse-drawn vehicle hadn't caught her snoring. Two trains, and now a stagecoach that had seen better days, had been enough to prove to her the inconveniences of traveling. How was a lady supposed to endure mile after mile of wheels jarring at every rut and fellow passengers snoring like an off-key church choir?

Sighing, she glanced down at the fawn colored material of her traveling suit and winced at the condition of the garment. When she'd purchased it two weeks ago, it had been one of the most stunning ensembles in the store, guaranteed by the saleswoman to travel with ease. Now the folds of fabric were wrinkled, covered with a layer of dust, and stained with coffee. Any positive first impressions she'd hoped to leave with her new employers were bound to be sadly lacking.

The man beside her, who oddly enough resembled the ruffian in her dream, shifted his weight, causing his elbow to gouge into her side. By the end of her journey to Browning City, she'd be bruised from head to toe, if not from the two men between whom she sat sandwiched, then from the rickety springs and constant bouncing of the stagecoach.

He nodded his apologies, then turned toward the small window overlooking endless miles of rolling hills and farmland. As the hours continued to pass, there had been little change in the scenery. Cornfields seemed to have swallowed up every inch of the fertile soil, interspersed by only an occasional farmhouse or apple orchard.

Iowa.

She knew little about the state except for stories from her aunt Rachel, and more recently, memories from the pages of her aunt's journal. A sudden bout with cholera may have taken her beloved aunt away from this world, but in her short lifetime, Rachel Young had traveled from San Francisco to

London and had seen more of this world than Tara might see if she lived to be a hundred.

A second glance at her attire brought a frown to her lips. Her aunt would have arrived at her destination in the height of fashion with barely a crease to show for her venture. Tara, on the other hand, seemed to have more in common with an Iowa farmer's wife than with a cultured lady. It was the latter role that had allowed her aunt to work above suspicion as she carried messages across enemy lines as a spy during the recent War Between the States. No one had anticipated Rachel Young to be anything other than a charming and beautiful socialite.

But expectations often ran sour. Tara stared at the heart-shaped stain on her skirt. Hadn't she always wanted to be like the other women in her family? Courageous and spirited. Even her parents, despite her mother's somewhat eccentric behavior, had worked for the Underground Railroad, helping dozens of slaves find freedom in the North, something President Ulysses S. Grant himself had attested to with a letter of recognition.

But most of the time she wasn't convinced it was even possible for a young woman of nineteen, as herself, to live up to the high standards that had been placed upon her.

"Miss Young?"

Mrs. Meddler's raspy voice brought Tara out of her reverie. A bright smile erupted across the face of the older woman who sat across from her. While Agnes Meddler's thin nose was too long and her brown gingham dress most unfashionable, at least she had been a pleasant source of conversation. The four men sharing the cramped quarters with them, on the other hand, had spent their time either sleeping or passing the bottle, much to Tara's disgust.

"Look outside." Mrs. Meddler jutted out her pointed chin. "We're almost there."

Tara strained her neck to look out the window. The dozing man beside her, his greased hair now plastered with dust, blocked most of the view, but if she stretched high enough she could catch a framed snippet of the terrain. The tops of the cornfields waved in the warm summer wind like a friendly greeting, but she could see no signs of houses or people or even Browning City.

Tara lowered her brow. "Are you sure we're almost there?"

"We're not more than a quarter of an hour away, I believe." The woman leaned forward in her seat and caught Tara's gaze. "No matter what anyone tells you, there's no better state than Iowa. Fruit trees, walnut trees, corn as far as the eye can see, and did you notice the lavender wildflowers? We call them wild bergamot, and they are but a sample of summer's colorful offering . . ."

Tara barely listened as the woman chattered on regarding the vast resources Iowa possessed and its good citizens. She hoped Browning City would boast something other than wildflowers, cornfields, and pleasant companions. While it might not offer all the cultural opportunities or the latest collections of fashionable clothing from Europe, she hoped it would at least offer a shaded city park or perhaps an ice cream parlor to provide a refreshing relief from the heat.

Of course, choosing to leave the comforts of the city had been her decision. Three weeks ago, she accepted the job as a companion for two of her distant elderly relatives, Thaddeus and Ginny Carpenter, in Browning City. But she hadn't taken the job for the income. Her aunt Rachel's journal mentioned a cache of gold lost by the Union army just waiting to be recovered — by her. She knew the Bible well enough to know that it was a sin to store up treasure here on earth, but this was different. This was her one chance to prove she could live up to her family's reputation and bear the Young name proudly.

When Mrs. Meddler hadn't been gossiping about how the sheriff had finally hired a deputy, or that the Dutch blacksmith and his wife recently had been surprised with twins, Tara had spent her time formulating her ideas to find the gold. And she was ready to put her plan into action.

Tara pressed her hand against her coiffed hair, wishing she had a chance to freshen up before alighting from the stage. A quick check with her fingers confirmed her suspicion that the combs had slipped beneath her velvet bonnet the saleslady had described as a regal shade of plum. And her skewed bonnet was no different from her misaligned life. Besides having the striking auburn color that ran in the Young family, she was the misfit who had never done anything that could even be considered courageous. Leaving the city to come to Iowa had been the first step to correct that image.

Fifteen minutes later, the stage came to a stop. Tara grasped the handle of her small beaded carpetbag, forcing herself to relax the tight muscles in her shoulders and still the flutter of butterflies in her stomach. She exchanged pleasantries with her short-term companions and disembarked with Mrs. Meddler while the driver unloaded their trunks.

From the edge of the station platform, she scanned the western horizon where the sun was already making its descent toward the rolling terrain. Mrs. Meddler had informed her that to the north lay the main street of town. Two dozen businesses, at the most, lined the wooden boardwalk, advertising their trade on hanging signs or hand painted on windowpanes. It was a far cry from Boston.

She tried to ignore her disappointment. "So this is Browning City?"

Mrs. Meddler laughed. "What did you expect? Chicago?"

Tara cleared her throat, wondering how the woman had managed to read her thoughts. "Of course not, but I . . . Really, it is beautiful with the sunlight shimmering through the clouds like a painted mural." She turned to her new friend. "And if the citizens are even half as nice as you say they are, then how could I not be happy here?"

Despite her sudden trepidation over the situation, Tara tried to sound convincing. The sky was beautiful, and she was glad to have a friend. Those two things, at least, were true.

"Will you be all right if I leave you now?" Worry shone through Mrs. Meddler's smile. "I do hate leaving you here all alone when you don't know a single soul in town besides me."

Tara gripped the handle of her bag. "Really, Mrs. Meddler. I'll be fine. Mr. Carpenter assured me that he would meet me here at the station, and I'm sure he will be along any minute."

At least, she hoped she was right. Surely her employer would be prompt when it came to time. After days of traveling, she wanted nothing more than a hot bath and a soft mattress on which to sleep. She'd then feel fresh enough tomorrow to put her plan into action.

Mrs. Meddler paused at the edge of the platform. "If by chance you do need to find me, just go into town and stop by the hotel and ask for me by name. It would be a pleasure to extend our visit over a cup of tea. Which, by the way, you must do once you are settled into your new position."

Tara smiled as the woman embraced her. "Thank you for your kindness, Mrs. Meddler. I'll take you up on the offer for tea one day soon."

Forty-five minutes later, Tara checked the

time on the gold locket she wore around her neck. Clearly she'd been wrong about two things. Not only was Browning City far from the bustling town she'd hoped for, Mr. Carpenter obviously had no sense of time. Both revelations made her uncomfortable. Except for the stationmaster, who'd disappeared around the back corner of the building a few minutes ago, the place was deserted.

After pulling a lace handkerchief from her bag, she wiped the moisture from her forehead. She hadn't counted on the weather being so humid. From the edge of the platform she looked down Main Street. Painted houses with picket fences skirted the edge of the town. She wondered what it would be like to live in such a quiet place. The Carpenters lived outside of town on a farm, meaning she'd be even more secluded. The very idea of being so isolated made her stomach clench.

"Excuse me, ma'am."

Tara spun around at the sound of a man's slurred voice.

"These here your trunks?"

"Yes, they are." When the driver had unloaded them from the stage and set them down, she'd seen no problem with where they'd been placed. She certainly wasn't in anyone's way. "Why do you ask?"

"No reason, except . . . you're a fine-looking woman." He took a step toward her.

Tara froze. Although he dressed as a cowboy, with denim jeans, chaps, and a bowler hat, there was no doubt in her mind that he was out to round up something other than cattle tonight. Sunlight caught the butt of a gun partially hidden inside his shirt.

Tara looked around, but the stationmaster was nowhere in sight. The knot in her stomach tightened. She measured the steps between them as he came closer. Five steps, maybe six? Why was it that in her dreams she was courageous and ready to face any challenge, but in real life all her instincts demanded she run the other direction?

She had to ponder the question only a fraction of a second. Deciding her trunks weren't worth her life, she bolted across the platform toward the dusty street, running until she felt the ironclad grip of the man's fingers encircle her arm.

Aaron Jefferson dismounted his horse, trying to brush away the past five hours of dust with a few measured sweeps of his hand. Nothing but a hot bath was going to get rid of all the grime he'd gathered from the long trek across the state.

Scanning the horizon, he worked to stretch out his legs and sore back muscles. Before him lay the same rolling hills he'd seen for the past three hundred miles. Or so it seemed. At least he'd made it to his destination. The sun would be setting in less than an hour, and all he wanted was a hearty meal and a good night's sleep before another full day's work tomorrow. A lame mount hadn't been on his schedule.

Aaron checked the front hoof of the mare and frowned as she flared her nostrils at him. The rambling station on the edge of Browning City was in view. Surely there'd be someone who could help him find a farrier to care for his horse, even at this hour.

This latest setback, though, seemed to be a simple quandary compared to the mounting pressure of his current government assignment. Patting his front pocket, he felt the folded letter of introduction and wondered if this town, like countless others before it, would prove to be nothing more than another wild goose chase. So far, none of his leads on the missing pile of Union army gold had gotten him any closer to the truth than when he first started. And Browning City was his last stop.

A scream rippled through the early

evening air. Tugging on the rim of his Stetson to block the piercing rays of sunlight that hovered on the edge of the horizon, he caught the silhouette of two people struggling on the station's platform. Instinct kicked in, and he ran toward the commotion. Ten yards closer made clear that there was a woman in trouble.

By the time he reached the bottom of the stairs, she'd managed to hit the man over the head with her handbag and break away from his grip. She glanced behind her before running straight toward Aaron. In the next instant, he caught a glimpse of skirts and petticoats flying at him as she stumbled down the platform stairs and into his arms.

He braced himself at the impact and struggled to keep his balance. "Are you all right, ma'am?"

"I think so." She hiccoughed and stared up at him with tear-rimmed eyes. "He grabbed me, and . . ."

The trickle turned into a flow of tears. He kept his arms around her waist to steady her, then glanced up at the man who'd assaulted her, not sure who he should deal with first. Outlaws he could handle. He'd dealt with ruffians, bank robbers, and even managed to hold his own in a gunfight or two. A panic-stricken woman was another bag of beans entirely.

He nodded toward the man who was still reeling from being clobbered in the head. "Do you know this scoundrel?"

Her face paled. "I've never seen him before in my life. I was waiting for someone when he came at me."

The man stumbled toward the top of the stairs, looking disoriented. Aaron took the steps two at a time until he came face-to-face with the woman's attacker. The smell of liquor permeated the man's breath. There was nothing Aaron hated more than a man showing disrespect to a woman, and he wasn't about to let this troublemaker get away with it.

The man tried to shove him away. "This ain't none of your business, mister. And besides, I was just trying to have some fun."

The muscles in Aaron's jaw tensed. "I don't know where you're from, but where I'm from, we don't treat our womenfolk this way."

The man tried to swing a punch at Aaron, but missed. Aaron placed one solid punch on the cowboy's jaw and laid him out flat on the wooden platform.

Aaron shook his hand and tried to ignore the sting across the back of his knuckles as he hurried back down the stairs. "You won't have to worry about him for a while."

She covered her lips with her gloved hands. "You punched him."

"I'm sorry, ma'am, but his intentions were quite obvious."

"Of course, it's just that . . ." She cleared her throat. "Thank you."

Aaron noticed the strands of auburn hair that peeked out of the woman's bonnet as she looked up at him. "Really, it was nothing. Nothing any other respectable man wouldn't do in the same circumstances . . ."

He let his jumbled words trail off, and for a moment, he saw nothing besides the clear depths of her gaze. Blue eyes peered out from behind long lashes, and he found himself staring into two of the most striking blue eyes he'd ever seen. She was pretty when she smiled. Beautiful, in fact. Aaron blinked and shook his head. Just because her skin was as smooth as porcelain and her lips full, and her figure . . . He turned away from her, putting a stop to the ridiculous thoughts. Since when did he fluster over a woman just because she happened to fall for him? Literally.

Aaron tugged on the brim of his Stetson. Something told him that he'd just stumbled on something far more dangerous than a stolen cache of gold.

# Two

Tara began to gather up the contents of her beaded bag, which had spilt across the ground when she'd whacked her assailant in the head. She wasn't sure what had just transpired between her and the handsome stranger standing beside her, but it was all she could do to keep her hands from trembling.

"What are we going to do with him?" She nodded at her attacker, who was slowly coming to.

"I'll handcuff him and take him to the sheriff." He dug into the pouch attached to his saddle and pulled out a pair of metal handcuffs.

Her eyes widened. "You're a lawman?"

"Something like that."

She wasn't surprised. He'd taken control of the situation as though it were an afternoon stroll in the park, while she, on the other hand, had managed to lose all sense of propriety and had panicked. As always. She shivered as she watched him take the stairs up to the station platform. Of course, her shaken nerves had nothing to do with the fact that she'd just gazed into the eyes of one of the most handsome men she'd ever seen. His eyes were brown, but not just any shade of brown. They were a rich toffee color with flecks of gold around the rims.

She shot another glance at him as he secured the prisoner's hands behind him. She barely saw the drunken cowboy. Instead, she noticed the lawman's coal black hair curled slightly around the nape of his neck. Stubble on his face gave him a rugged look, but the gentleness she'd seen in his eyes caused her pulse to quicken. She picked up her handkerchief, now covered with dust, crammed it into her bag, and bit her lip. Her rescuer's solid stature and strong jawline certainly weren't the reasons her heart was pounding. No, it had to be from the drunken man who'd left bruises on her forearms.

"I shouldn't have panicked." She grabbed the last item and shoved it into the bag, speaking her thoughts aloud. "I should have held my head up and demanded he leave me alone."

"Pretty hard to do with a man who's not

only twice your size but also drunk. You had every right to be afraid." He dragged his prisoner to his feet. "And hitting him over the head with your bag took a bit of courage if you ask me."

Tara frowned. There was a big difference between courage and reacting out of sheer terror. Clutching her bag with one hand, she tried to straighten her bonnet, which was now completely askew. "I thought I left behind the high crime of the city, but I must have been mistaken."

He led the man down the stairs. "Where are you from? Des Moines?"

"No. Boston, actually."

"Unfortunately there's a bad egg in every lot whether you're in Boston, Philadelphia . . . or Browning City, Iowa." His grin left a dimple on his right cheek. "Let me be the first to properly welcome you, as most Iowans would, and assure you that not all of us are like this ruffian. Some of us are actually quite . . . well . . . quite nice."

"I'm sure you must be right." A shadow crossed the man's face, erasing his pleasant smile, and she wondered if she'd said something to offend him. "So you live here?"

"Originally, though I haven't lived here for a number of years."

"Then I'd say we've both had quite an interesting welcome to Browning City."

He raised his Stetson and scratched his head. "Can I take you somewhere? I don't think it's safe for you to be here alone."

"That has become perfectly clear. But I . . ." Tara paused. Where should she go? She could take up Mrs. Meddler's hospitable offer and stay the night at the hotel. But what would Mr. Carpenter think when he eventually showed up, and she wasn't at the station? If he showed up at all.

She turned at the sound of a squeaky wagon coming toward the station. "Perhaps that's Mr. Carpenter now."

"For your sake, I certainly hope so."

A moment later, the wagon pulled up beside her, and a man who looked to be as old as Moses stepped on the brake. "Miss Young?"

"Yes. Mr. Carpenter?"

"Welcome to Browning City, young lady. It's mighty good to see you." His wrinkled face was swallowed up by a toothless grin as he slapped his hands against his thighs. "And right on time, I might add."

"Right on time?" Tara's eyes widened in surprise.

"As always." Mr. Carpenter pulled a gold watch out of his pocket and flipped it open.

"Five o'clock on the dot. Last stage pulls through here at this time three days a week."

"But Mr. Carpenter, it's well past five —"

"A fine piece of work, isn't it?" He stared at the engraved picture on the outside of the watch. "My father bought this beauty in London before immigrating to America in 1793. Gave it to me on my sixteenth birthday, only two weeks before he was killed by a bull in our back pasture."

"Oh my. I . . . I'm sorry." Tara glanced at her toffee-eyed hero, who looked to be as taken aback as she was by the eccentric man in denim overalls and a starched shirt.

"Not to worry," Mr. Carpenter said. "That was over five decades ago, I'd say, and a body has to eventually go on with his life."

"I suppose you're right." Tara quickly calculated the man's age. She knew her grandmother's second cousin had been older, but this man had to be close to seventy. "In any case, it is good to finally meet you."

"Hop into the wagon then. My Ginny has chicken-fried steak and mashed potatoes on the stove and hates it when I'm late for supper."

Tara's mouth watered. Hopefully Mrs. Carpenter's cooking was better than her husband's sense of time. She paused, glancing at the platform. "I do have two trunks."

"I've got 'em."

Mr. Carpenter nodded his thanks to the lawman, who picked up the first one and set it in the wagon bed. "Sampson will take care of them once we get to the farm."

Tara fiddled with one of the beads on her bag, wondering if she dared ask the obvious question. "Who's Sampson?"

"A fine man, he is. Lost his hearing in one ear when a cannon exploded beside him during the war, but other than that, the man's in perfect health. A good thing now that my Ginny and I are getting a bit up in years." He pulled out a handkerchief from his pocket and blew his nose. "Canning pickles tomorrow."

"Sampson is?" Tara shook her head, trying to follow the conversation while her trunks were being loaded.

"Of course not. The missus. She thought you might enjoy such a task. Nothing like a crisp, firm pickle."

Pickles? Tara scrunched up her nose. Did she dare tell her new employer that the only pickled fare she'd ever tasted had come straight from her grocer's shelves? She'd understood her job description to be more refined, like answering correspondence, reading pages from Charlotte Brontë or

Henry David Thoreau, and perhaps a bit of simple cooking. Pickles weren't included in her definition of a cultured supper or dinner.

Tara climbed up into the wagon, wondering if she'd been a bit hasty coming to Iowa. Certainly finding the stash of gold would be worth any inconvenience, but beside the fact that Thaddeus Carpenter happened to be her grandmother's cousin, it occurred to her how little she knew about the man and his wife.

"Been some trouble?" Mr. Carpenter pointed a bony finger at the prisoner who lay hunched over on the stairs. "You must be the new deputy."

"He's not the new deputy." She sat down on the hard seat. "But that man tried to attack me, and this other gentleman came to my rescue. He's a lawman."

"Then I appreciate your kindness, sir." Mr. Carpenter handed Tara the reins and slowly started to climb out of the wagon. "I'd like to get down and shake your hand for taking care of this young woman."

Something cracked in the old man's joints. Tara winced as she watched him ease his way toward the side of the wagon.

"Mr. Carpenter . . ." Her voice trailed off

as he slowly lifted one leg to the edge of the wagon.

"Sorry, but I'm not near as spry as I was a few years ago. Takes me a bit of time."

"Please, don't worry about getting down." With his Stetson between his hands, the stranger hurried over to the wagon to shake Mr. Carpenter's hand. "The trunks are in the back of the wagon, and I'm headed for the sheriff's office. No doubt this young woman is ready to get home."

"Once again, then, we're in your debt." Mr. Carpenter took the reins once more and winked at Tara. "I'd say it's time to get home, missy."

Hanging on to the edge of the seat with her fingertips for balance, Tara braced herself as the horses started down the dirt road at a steady trot. She turned back to take one last look at the lawman who'd rescued her as they made their way out of town and realized she'd forgotten to ask him his name.

Aaron escorted his prisoner through the doorway of the sheriff's office, thankful the woman's attacker was too drunk to have put up a real fight. He knew he was far too tired to deal with the scoundrel.

"What have we got here?"

At the sheriff's question, Aaron shoved the prisoner into a wooden chair and stepped up to the sheriff's desk. The uniformed lawman sat with an apple in one hand and a newspaper in the other, apparently feeling as if there was little need for him to be patrolling the streets of this cozy community.

"My name's Aaron Jefferson. I've got a letter of introduction."

He handed the bearded man the letter. The sheriff lowered his glasses to the tip of his nose and peered over the top of the octagonal lenses. "Says here you're working for the United States government."

"Yes, sir." Aaron rotated the brim of his Stetson in his hands. "Hadn't meant to meet you under these circumstances, but not only is this man drunker than a passed-out coon, he attacked a woman tonight at the station."

The sheriff gave a cursory glance at the accused before setting down the letter. "Bud Pickett's about as harmless as they come. All talk and no action."

Aaron shook his head. "Not this time. He's drunk, and I'm certain he left marks on the woman's arms."

"Bud, what have you gone and done?"

Bud banged his head against the brick

wall behind him. "I ain't done nothing but try and talk to a woman. Nothing against the law about that, is there, Sheriff Morton?"

"It is when you grab her and scare the living daylights out of her," Aaron countered.

"I said, I's just trying to talk to her, but then he comes and handcuffs me like I'm some criminal."

Aaron rocked back on his heels. "There happens to be a big difference between talking and attacking —"

"All right, enough, you two." The sheriff held up his hand. "Normally I wouldn't take kindly to someone cuffing up one of my citizens and dragging him in here, but if you're telling the truth, Mr. Jefferson, I suppose you didn't have a choice. Now, what was the woman's name?"

Aaron stared at the wanted poster hanging behind the sheriff's desk and drew a blank. Had he even asked her? Surely he'd remember something as simple as whether or not he'd asked for her name. He lived his life paying attention to detail and drawing information from people without them knowing what he was doing. He stroked his chin and felt its rough stubble. Obviously, blue eyes and long, dark lashes had not only left him tongue-tied, they had rendered him

31

temporarily senseless as well.

He rested his hands against the desk and leaned forward. "I . . . I don't know what her name was."

"You don't know her name?" The sheriff balanced his chair on its back legs and eyed him warily. "And how do you propose I follow up on this incident when you don't even know the name of the woman involved? Seems like for a lawman you're a bit lacking in your investigative skills."

Aaron's fists tightened at the comment. "She's staying with the Carpenters on a farm outside of town."

The sheriff nodded and set his glasses down on the desk before rubbing his eyes. "Ol' Thaddeus Carpenter and his wife Ginny. Heard they had some relative coming from the big city. Hope she knows something about farmwork and making pickles."

"Pickles?" Aaron leaned forward. "Why's that?"

"Don't get me wrong, we all love the couple, but Thaddeus can be quite a character. I hope she knows what she's getting into."

One didn't have to be a genius to pick up on the fact that Mr. Carpenter might have been a bit senile, but he also couldn't quite picture the man's newly hired help canning pickles and assisting with the farm chores. While her dress might have been a bit weathered from the trip, she certainly hadn't bought it at a small town mercantile. She'd been poised and educated, and he was quite certain that the woman had been raised as anything but an Iowan farm girl.

Aaron cleared his throat. "You're kidding me, right?"

"And why would I do that?"

"I don't know, I just . . ." He shook his head. It wasn't his place to worry about someone he hadn't even properly met. "Never mind. Listen, I've been on the trail all day and need a bite to eat and a good night's sleep. If you don't mind taking care of Mr. Pickett —"

"Not at all. I'll keep him here overnight so he can sleep it off."

Aaron put his hat back on and turned to leave. "Good night, then."

Shoving his hands into his pockets, he left the sheriff's office, disturbed over his own behavior. For a man intent on leaving a professional impression, he'd certainly messed up this time.

No matter what his usual resolve, his brief encounter with the young woman had left him daydreaming of auburn hair and striking blue eyes. In the past, he'd never had trouble ignoring most women, spending his time, instead, putting everything he had into his assignments. And certainly no woman had ever gotten in the way of career. He had no time for love and courtship. Maybe one day, when he'd finally proved he was just as competent as his father and his father's father, he'd settle down and start a family. Until then, he'd stick to chasing down leads for the United States government. Besides, most of the pretty girls he managed to meet weren't exactly the kind he imagined himself marrying.

*Until tonight.*

Aaron kicked at a loose rock on the boardwalk, even more determined to put the fair lady out of his mind. He hurried down the street toward the hotel. Ten thousand dollars in gold lay somewhere between here and the Mississippi River, and all a woman would do would be to get him into trouble. No, Mr. Carpenter's newly hired help could stick to making pickles and slopping the hogs for all he cared. He had to get back to work.

# THREE

Tara groaned at the insistent knocking on her bedroom door. She rolled to her side, drawing the covers over her head. Light had barely begun to filter through the window, and she had no plans of rising before the sun did. She rolled onto her back and frowned. Something was wrong. The bed was lumpy, the sheets were scratchy . . .

The past few days came rushing to her like a whirlwind. Her long trip to Iowa, Mr. and Mrs. Carpenter, and the cramped room on the second floor that would be hers as long as she stayed with them. She yawned, willing whoever was at her door to go away. She'd spent half the night tossing and turning on the uncomfortable mattress, and the other half dreaming about the handsome lawman rescuing her from the hands of a ruthless villain.

Someone knocked again.

"Miss Young?" Mrs. Carpenter called to her.

Tara sat up, trying to determine if she'd heard an edge of panic in the older woman's voice. What if one of them was sick? Nursing had not been one of the requirements for the job she'd taken.

She pulled the covers up under her chin. "Is something wrong?"

Mrs. Carpenter seemed to take her question as an invitation, because she crept into the room, moving directly to tug back the patterned curtains hanging along a small window. "I do hope you got a good night's sleep, Miss Young, because it's going to be a beautiful day."

Tara frowned and glanced out the window tinged with the faint light of dawn. Besides its pale yellow glow, the only other light came from the candle stub the woman held. Certainly these farm people didn't actually rise before dawn.

Tara worked to stretch a kink in her neck. "What time is it?"

"Five thirty." Light from the candle flickered across the older woman's face, catching her widening smile. A rooster cried out in the distance, but other than that, the morning lay shrouded in a canopy of stillness. "Thaddeus and I always rise by five,

36

but I let you sleep in a bit today, as I know you must be tired from your long journey."

Tired from her long journey? As if that were even in question. Tara had just spent the past four days battling overloaded trains and coaches, sick passengers, and bad food, and now Mrs. Carpenter wanted her to jump out of bed and face the world before she'd had sufficient time to catch her breath.

"I am a bit tired." Pulling the edge of the thin quilt around her, she worked to keep the frustration out of her voice.

In all good conscience, it wasn't Mrs. Carpenter's fault that Tara's expectations of living on a farm had been too optimistic. Such a place could never compare to the modern conveniences of her home in Boston, where they had amenities like piped-in water and an indoor necessary. Perhaps she'd simply always taken for granted her own amply stuffed feather bed and linen sheets along with the many other things farm life obviously lacked.

Tara stifled another yawn. "I'm just not used to waking quite so early."

"Don't you worry about a thing, dear." Mrs. Carpenter tugged on the top of her mobcap, with its puffed crown and ribbon trim — a fashion that should have been disregarded decades ago, in Tara's opinion.

37

"You'll get used to it. Early rising is good for a body. You'll sleep better at night, as well."

Tara bit her tongue at the string of complaints that threatened to erupt, trying instead to focus her mind on what her Aunt Rachel had taught her from the Bible. *He that is slow to anger is better than the mighty; and he that ruleth his spirit than he that taketh a city.* Or in her case, better a woman who doesn't complain about a little hard work and lack of sleep than one who loses all sense of propriety while attempting to uncover a lost fortune of gold for the United States government. Pulling her robe around her shoulders, she sent up a short prayer that God would find it within Himself to grant her both an extra measure of patience *and* the cache of gold.

Mrs. Carpenter set the candle on a dresser covered with framed daguerreotypes, bric-a-brac, and a thick layer of dust. "I've got breakfast on the stove. Didn't want you to have to worry about that on your first morning here. Then we've got a busy day ahead of us. We're in the middle of pickling, you know."

Pickles? Mr. Carpenter had been serious?

Five hours, six hundred pickles, and countless pots of boiling water later, Mrs. Carpenter suggested they stop for a meal of ham, beans, biscuits, and a sampling of a previous batch of their homemade pickles. Tara tried to hide her aversion to the cured cucumber, quite certain she had no desire to look at another pickle let alone eat another one as long as she lived.

Mr. Carpenter's wooden chair squeaked beneath him as he sat down at the dinner table, causing Tara to wonder if it would hold up under the man's slight weight. Like the Carpenters, everything in the white-washed farmhouse was old-fashioned, shabby, and worn. The walls were covered with faded paint; the mahogany furniture, with its carved feathers and eagle medallion ornamentation, most certainly came from another century. Even the cookstove was an outmoded cast-iron beast that was slower than yesterday's stagecoach.

Mr. Carpenter stabbed a piece of ham with his fork. "I was wondering if you could do me a favor this afternoon, Miss Young."

Tara fidgeted in her seat across from him. She had hoped that her duties would be minimal, giving her time to follow up the clues in her aunt's diary, but she was beginning to fear that wasn't going to be the case.

She forced a smile. "Of course. I'd be

happy to do anything you need me to."

He helped himself to a second serving of beans while his wife fluttered in and out of the kitchen making sure they had everything they needed. "The post office was closed by the time I went to fetch you last night, and I have a letter that needs to be mailed."

Tara wiped the corners of her mouth with a cloth napkin, wondering if she'd just received the answer to her prayer. "And you'd like me to take it into town?"

Mrs. Carpenter sat down at the table, a second jar of opened pickles in her hand. "It's an easy drive into town, but the wagon is hard on poor Thaddeus's joints."

For the first time all morning, Tara's smile was genuine. "I'd be delighted to help. I'll have to change my clothes and freshen up a bit first —"

"Of course, my dear." She exchanged glances with her husband. "There are a few eligible bachelors in town, and I remember how important it was to make a good impression as a young woman who had yet to step into the joys of matrimony."

Tara scooted her chair back and shook her head. "Oh, but I didn't come here to find a man to court me. I came here to . . ." She stopped herself before the word *gold* slipped off her tongue. "To work for you, of course."

Mrs. Carpenter reached out and patted her hand. "Just don't be thinking that we won't give you any time off. We know how important it is for young people to enjoy themselves."

Mr. Carpenter nudged his wife with his bony elbow. "If I'm not mistaken, our Miss Young has already found herself a possible suitor. Remember I told you last night that a stranger saved her from a drunken scoundrel at the station?"

Tara gasped. "Why, I don't even know who that man was —"

"You did mention to me that he was handsome, Thaddeus." Mrs. Carpenter cocked her head and smiled. "Ahh, new love. There's nothing sweeter."

Tara shook her head. "I really don't think —"

"Don't mind my dear wife, Miss Young. She's a bit of a romantic, I must say, and she always manages to find a way to play matchmaker, don't you, dear? After fifty years of marriage, I suppose she simply wishes the same happiness we've found on others."

Tara closed her mouth. The last thing she wanted in her life right now was her own private matchmaker, but it was obvious she wasn't going to get a word in edgewise. She watched as Mrs. Carpenter leaned toward her husband and whispered something in his ear. He caught her hand and laughed.

"My wife just reminded me of our own courting days." Mr. Carpenter's gaze never left his wife's face. "Ah, the good Lord was gracious to bring us together. He may not have ever blessed us with children, but He's allowed us to live out our days on this earth together."

Tara crushed the napkin between her fingers, as something stirred within her. The love between the Carpenters was obvious, and she couldn't help but find herself growing attached to this odd yet endearing couple. Her own parents loved her, but they spent most of their time running the family business and staying involved in various patriotic activities.

With the last bite of her meal gone, Tara washed the dishes and changed her clothes before heading toward the barn. Making her way gingerly across the hay-strewn shelter, she once again questioned her sanity for coming to Iowa. At home, she would have stepped out the front door of her house and straight into an awaiting carriage. But Browning City was a far cry from Boston.

At least she'd been taught how to drive a wagon back in Boston and wasn't completely helpless. Even riding had been done with little effort, though, as the stable boys would get the horses ready for her. Holding her gloved fingers against her nose, she followed the cheerful whistles of Sampson, who was cleaning out one of the stalls with a wide smile on his ebony face.

"Mr. Sampson?"

The man continued his tune, seemingly oblivious to the fact that she was calling him. She'd almost forgotten. The farmhand was partially deaf. She regarded the dusty floor and raised the hem of her skirt an extra inch for good measure before taking another step closer.

Tara eyed the pale mare in front of her and raised her voice. "Mr. Sampson?"

The horse's head jerked toward her and its ears laid flat. Tara stumbled backward and slammed into a wooden post.

"Miss Young . . ." Sampson held up his hand to stop her before approaching the animal with quiet, soothing words.

He stroked the horse's shoulder and turned to Tara. "Horses scare easy, miss. Never come near 'em from behind. You're liable to startle them."

Tara stared down at her handbag. "I'm sorry. I —"

"And always make sure the horse sees ya

before comin' near. They ain't aggressive, but they does frighten easy." He looked at her and smiled. "Don't worry, miss. After a few weeks of livin' here, it'll be easy for ya."

Tara grasped the edge of the post behind her, feeling foolish. There was no hiding the fact that she was a city girl. Even from an uneducated farmhand.

She cleared her throat and raised her chin. "Mr. Carpenter wanted me to go into town for him. I have driven a wagon before."

Sampson's broad smile showed off his white teeth. "Give me five minutes, miss."

"Thank you, Sampson."

The broad-shouldered man set down his shovel and went back to whistling his tune. Strange how a man could appear so happy when his job was nothing more than mucking stalls and working in the field.

True to his word, Sampson had the wagon hitched and ready in a few short minutes. Perched on the narrow bench, Tara was overcome with a feeling of freedom for the first time since leaving Boston. The pungent smell of vinegar that had permeated the Carpenters' kitchen as they poured the boiling brine over the dozens of green cucumbers was now replaced with the faint scent of wildflowers that dotted the landscape as she headed toward town.

Tara smiled. Her aunt's journal was tucked safely in her bag, and she was finally ready to put the first part of her plan into action. Armed with the name of one of her aunt's informants, she was determined to track down the whereabouts of the missing gold.

She reached up to ensure that her summer garden hat, with its spray of flowers, was perched securely atop her head. Feeling the need for an extra measure of confidence, she'd chosen to wear one of her favorite dresses, a gray poplin walking dress trimmed with two flounces and paired with a matching short jacket edged with lilac trim. Making a good impression on the sheriff was the first step in her plan to extract the necessary information from the lawman. Honesty, beauty, and a bit of womanly charm had always proven to be a highly persuasive combination.

Twenty minutes later, she stood in front of the sheriff's office. Taking a deep breath, she stepped inside. The sheriff sat at his desk, engrossed in a stack of papers.

Tara cleared her throat and stepped up to the small room that wasn't even half the size of her sitting area back home. "I'm sorry to disturb you, Sheriff."

The middle-aged man looked up, rubbing

his graying beard with his fingertips. "Sheriff Morton. Good afternoon."

The lawman stood, knocking over his chair in the process. He stumbled to pick it up, then scattered the pile of papers with his elbow. "Excuse me, please, I . . . I'm not usually quite this clumsy." A dark tint of red covered the man's cheeks as he hurried to pick the papers up.

Once he had collected the items and placed them back on his desk, she reached out and shook his hand. "My name is Tara Young, and I can't begin to say how pleased I am to meet you, Sheriff Morton."

"Really?" Fiddling with his pencil, the man sat back down and peered at her over the top of his octagonal lenses. "Please have a seat. The pleasure is definitely all mine."

She sent him her most flattering smile. "Thank you."

"You're from out of town?"

"I'm from back east, actually, Boston. I just arrived in town last night."

"Then you must be the Carpenters' relative who's come to help them out."

Tara's brows rose. "I see that word spreads quickly in a small town like Browning City."

"That is one of the potential drawbacks of living in such a quiet community, but to most of us, the advantages far outweigh the disadvantages." The sheriff laughed. "What can I do for you?"

Tara clutched her bag against her chest. "I know you must be terribly busy with your work protecting the good citizens of this town —"

"Please." He held up a hand of protest. "Don't worry. There's always time to assist a beautiful young woman such as yourself."

"You're too kind." Tara leaned forward and lowered her voice. "Since you are a man of the law, I hope I can be assured of your complete confidentiality in what I'm going to ask you."

The sheriff removed his glasses and raised his thick brows. "But of course. I wouldn't be able to uphold the law if I was a man who couldn't keep confidences, now would I?"

Tara nodded. "I'm happy to hear you say that, because what I need to discuss with you is rather . . . delicate to say the least."

He set his pencil down. "I'm listening."

Confident she now had the man's full attention, Tara continued. "My aunt, who sadly passed away suddenly last year, worked as a spy for the North during the recent War Between the States, and in reading through her journal, I came across some entries that, well, I simply couldn't ignore."

"Entries about what?"

"A cache of gold stolen from the Union army that is rumored to be buried somewhere in the area."

Sheriff Morton leaned back in his chair and let out a deep belly laugh. "I hate to disappoint you, Miss Young, but I've heard more rumors about that missing gold than there are jackrabbits in our cornfields. Not too many years back a woman arrived in town who believed her father had a role in the heist, but no pot of gold ever turned up. Even the government claims that it exists, but I've been sheriff here for nearly thirty years, and I can promise you that if you go after that gold around here, you're only going to be chasing ghosts. There's no gold. Least not in my territory."

Tara ignored the sting of disappointment, but she wasn't finished yet. "I've got a name."

The sheriff cocked his head and eyed her warily. "A name? What do you mean?"

"My aunt mentions a man named Schlosser in connection to the gold."

"Schlosser. Richart Schlosser." He rubbed his beard. "If I remember correctly, Mr. Schlosser moved away three or four years ago. Lived on a farm a few miles out of town. All I can suggest to you is that you

48

talk to the land agent and see if he has an exact record of when the family lived here. But if you ask me, you're better off spending your time caring for the Carpenters rather than chasing some alleged pot of gold."

Tara frowned at the man's last comment. Beauty and charm might give her an advantage at times, but it seemed they did little to ensure one was taken seriously. She stood and stepped behind the chair. It was time to end their conversation.

"I do appreciate greatly your taking the time to talk with me about this, Sheriff."

"I'm at your service any time, Miss Young." He stood and moved to the edge of his desk where he tapped his fingers against the hardwood. "There is one other thing, I almost forgot. I have the man who attacked you last night locked up in the jail. He's slept off his stupor, and I've given him a thorough lecture. Unless you feel compelled to press charges . . ."

"No, please." The last thing she wanted to do was make an incident out of the situation. "I think I'd rather put the entire episode behind me."

Tara nodded her thanks, then stepped out onto the boardwalk. While she was embarrassed over her reaction toward the drunken man and would rather forget the discomfiting moment — except perhaps the encounter with the handsome stranger — she was even more disappointed about the sheriff's reaction to the gold. Of course, she wasn't certain what she had been expecting. At least the visit wasn't completely in vain. She'd seen the land agent's office on the outskirts of town, and would take the time to inquire after the whereabouts of Mr. Schlosser once she delivered Mr. Carpenter's letter.

Tara crossed the street toward the post office, careful to avoid the patches of black mud that filled the street. She secured her hat with one hand as a gust of wind tried to blow it off her head. The last thing she needed was her summer hat to end up with a thick coating of Iowa mud.

At the edge of the boardwalk, an envelope fluttered to the ground in front of her. She caught it, then searched to find its owner. Her heart thumped as she looked up into the toffee brown eyes of the handsome stranger who had rescued her the night before.

Aaron gazed into the familiar face of the woman who'd filled his dreams the night before, and he somehow managed to stammer an awkward, "good morning."

Her bubbly laugh sounded as light as the tinkling of a bell. "It's already afternoon."

"Of course." Aaron frowned, feeling suddenly foolish over his obvious display of nerves.

She held up one of his letters that had blown out of his hands. "Is this yours?"

He took the envelope, allowing the tips of their fingers to touch in the exchange. "Thank you. I was on my way to post the letters and there was a gust of wind . . ."

For a moment, an awkward pause hovered between them. Of course, she knew that. Aaron swallowed hard, wishing he didn't feel quite so happy to see her. With his information coming straight from Washington, his arrival in Browning City had been planned out in detail. He was to arrive, spend the morning mapping out the town and its occupants, visit with the sheriff, then interview those he felt might have information regarding the events that led up to the disappearance of the gold five years ago. His itinerary didn't include falling for the first beautiful woman he encountered. Not that he'd actually fallen for her. But it was true that he hadn't stopped thinking about her.

He tapped the envelopes against the palm

of his hand. "I hadn't expected to see you again."

She lifted the edge of her skirt and stepped onto the boardwalk. "Actually, since Browning City is no metropolitan center, I would think that the odds of us running into each other were actually quite high."

"True." He took off his Stetson and followed her toward the post office. "I wanted to apologize for not introducing myself properly last night. With all the commotion, it seems as if I completely forgot my manners."

She stopped, turning to face him as a slight blush crept up her cheeks. "It's only natural that the formalities would get pressed aside in such a situation."

The explosion of a gunshot ripped through the afternoon air as a bullet ricocheted off the painted sign above their heads. Aaron grabbed her arm and shoved her through the doorway of the post office out of the line of fire.

# FOUR

"Are you all right?"

Tara nodded as she stared into the face of the man who had managed to prevent her from harm for a second time in twenty-four hours. She crouched inside, beneath the window of the post office, willing the shots to subside. Someone screamed. The window shattered above them, sending thick shards of glass across the wooden floor.

"Fear thou not; for I am with thee. Fear thou not; for I am with thee . . ." She repeated the scripture over and over, mumbling the words aloud.

Aaron crouched next to her, leaning on his palms. "Isaiah chapter forty-one?"

She nodded at his question, surprised he knew the verse. "So you believe in God?"

"Especially at moments like this." He pulled his gun out of his holster and checked the barrel. "I've faced death a time or two in my life and know that I don't want to leave this world without the hope of spending eternity with Him."

A gun fired again, exploding through the afternoon air like a blast of dynamite. Tara struggled to breathe. While she, too, believed as a Christian that the good Lord would one day take her home to live with Him forever, she hadn't expected that moment to be now. There were still a few things she wanted to take care of on this side of eternity first.

She lowered her head and tried to take a handful of slow, deep breaths. Aunt Rachel would have strutted out the front door of the post office and given the gunman a severe tongue-lashing for his disrupting the afternoon of the good citizens of this town. Her father would have found a way to disarm the man before marching him to the sheriff's office. She, on the other hand, was ready to hang up her fiddle and run. If the odds weren't so overwhelmingly high that she would get shot in the process, she had half a mind to do just that.

The lawman beside her lifted her chin with his thumb and caught her anxious gaze. "It's going to be all right, you know."

His calm voice washed over her like a soothing balm. She stared into his toffee eyes and wished she could transport this moment to another place in time. He gazed back at her, and she wanted to believe that what he said was true. His lips curled into a smile, and her stomach flipped. She turned away, fiddling with one of the beads on her bag. How could she entertain thoughts of romance when any minute a bullet could ricochet off the brick wall, signaling the end to one or both of their lives?

Still crouched, she wrapped her arms around herself and rocked back on the heels of her lace-up boots. "How do you know everything's going to be all right?"

"Trust me."

The silence that followed was as loud as the screams and gunfire that had permeated the afternoon seconds before. Tara held her breath. No one moved. It was as if time hovered between them, not wanting to go forward and uncover the final dreadful moment of the standoff.

The lawman signaled her with his hand. "Come with me."

He hurried her behind the counter of the post office, where three other women and two men sat huddled against the wall. One of the women cried silently, while another one simply stared straight ahead, her face void of expression.

He reached out and grasped Tara's hand.

"You'll be all right here. I've got to stop him."

"No!" Tara's eyes widened. She tugged at his sleeve as he moved to leave. "He'll kill you."

"I'll be fine. I'm a lawman, remember?" He squeezed her hand. "And besides, I'm hanging on to those words from Isaiah."

Tara clenched her jaw together as he crept around the counter. God might be with them, but that certainly didn't always stop bad things from happening. And if he got shot . . .

She tried to steady her rapid breathing, but instead her pulse raced even quicker. The whole situation was ridiculous. Here she was caught in the cross fire of some madman, terrified something was going to happen to a complete stranger. She didn't even know his name. Pressing her back against the wall, she squeezed her eyes closed and tried to ignore the whispers of the others huddling beside her. How could it be that instead of a quiet town among the rolling hills, fruit trees, and cornfields of Iowa, she seemed to have landed in America's treacherous frontier?

She chewed on the edge of her lip. The whole reason she'd left her parents' home and moved here was to prove to herself that she could handle a challenge . . . that she wasn't the spoiled rich girl some of her acquaintances had accused her of being . . . that she wasn't the terrified individual who was right now sitting in a volatile situation about to faint from fear.

Someone shouted.

Her fingernails bit into her palms as she squeezed her hands shut. She had to know what was happening. He had saved her life. She wouldn't let him die in some futile attempt to hold on to his honor.

Keeping her head below the top of the wooden counter, she gathered up the thick folds of her dress material in one hand and scooted across the floor. One of the older women reached out and tugged on the waist of her skirt.

"What in the world do you think you are doing, miss?"

Tara glanced back at the woman. "I've got to know what's happening. He's —"

"This is not a time for curiosity." A scowl crossed the older woman's face. "All you can do right now is pray that man of yours doesn't do something foolish and get himself killed."

Her man? Tara frowned. That certainly was far from the truth, but it didn't matter at the moment. She knew exactly how high his chances were for getting killed, and she didn't need to be reminded of the danger into which he'd put himself.

Ignoring the woman's unmistakable gestures to stay put, Tara continued to ease her way across the floor until she could peek around the edge of the counter. His Stetson lay discarded on the floor. Her foot crunched on a piece of glass. With her skirts gathered in one hand and her other hand pressed against the wall to keep her balance, she quickly picked up the hat and placed it on her own bonnet before continuing carefully toward the broken window.

A splinter of glass pierced through the delicate material of her glove, leaving a crimson stain on the white surface. Ignoring the sting, she pulled out the offending fragment, determined to tread more carefully across the floor. She'd deal with the blemished article of clothing later.

Once she reached the corner, she pressed her back against the brick wall and strained her neck to make out what was going on. From her new vantage point, she could see out onto the street and to the other side of the boardwalk that had been abandoned by dozens of early afternoon shoppers.

A man dressed in black pointed his gun to the sky and took another shot. She scanned her limited view through the framed window for a sign of the lawman. There was movement to her left. Finally, she caught sight of him. He was crouching behind a display of vegetables out in front of the mercantile, waiting his next move. The gunman let out a string of profanities. Tara covered her ears, then froze as the lawman stealthily moved across the boardwalk toward the street. A plank of wood groaned beneath his weight. The gunman whirled around and aimed his weapon.

Tara screamed, then everything went black.

Aaron flinched at the deafening scream that pierced the humid afternoon air. The barrel of the gun that had been aimed at him a moment ago jerked to the left as the man turned to find the source of the scream. Being convinced the gunman was as crazy as a loon and wouldn't hear his approach had been Aaron's first mistake. But the gunman's last move had just sealed his fate. All Aaron had needed was a two-second distraction to be able to restrain the man from injuring any innocent bystander. The scream had given him just that.

In four quick strides, Aaron reached the man. He secured the gun first, throwing it out of arm's reach, then tackled the felon to the ground before the man had the opportunity to react to what had hit him. The gunman twisted around and threw a punch, skimming his knuckles across Aaron's jaw. But Aaron had a good six inches on the man as well as extra muscle, and in a matter of seconds he had the man subdued.

With his knee against the man's back, Aaron pushed away the blue-eyed vision that appeared in front of him, wondering if it had been her ruse that had saved his life. Another second later, if the gunman had any sense of accuracy, the bullet would have hit its mark and gone straight through his heart.

"Why didn't you just shoot him?"

Aaron turned and looked up at the rider behind him. The sheriff dismounted from his stallion and folded his arms across his chest.

Aaron rubbed his jaw, thankful the man hadn't broken it. "I'm not the killing kind. Try to avoid it at all costs."

"Even at the cost of your own life?" The lawman stepped forward and rolled the gunman over onto his back. "Either way, it looks as if I'm in your debt once again, Mr. Jefferson."

"I just happened to be at the right place

at the right time."

"If I'm not mistaken, I've got a wanted poster for this rogue." The man tried to sit up, but the sheriff pushed him back down with the heel of his boot. "I appreciate your quick thinking. Any chance you might be looking for a job as deputy? My new one just quit on me."

Aaron shook his head. "Thanks kindly for the offer, but I believe I've got enough on my plate at the moment."

"Working for the government, I suppose you would."

Aaron hauled the gunman to his feet. "But I would be happy to escort this man to the jail for you."

The front of Aaron's plaid shirt and denim jeans were covered with dust, and he'd lost his Stetson somewhere in the process. Glancing at the wooden sign hanging above the jail across the street, he had to wonder what kind of sheriff ran such an unruly town.

If he hadn't known better, he might have thought he'd missed his mark and showed up in the lawless town of Abilene. Not that gunfights were uncommon. In decades past, learned men might have been excused for taking part in duels, but he drew the line at ruffians shooting innocent citizens in the streets.

He turned back to the post office and caught a flash of gray material through the broken window. He wondered if it was her. He still smelled the soft fragrance of her perfume, remembered every detail of her face, and could, even now, feel the softness of her skin when he'd briefly touched her jawline. And he didn't even know her name.

Part of him longed to go after her. To properly introduce himself and discover more about her. He had a dozen questions he wanted to ask . . . But now was not the time to go chasing after some beautiful woman who'd somehow managed to capture a corner of his heart. She'd be fine, and he'd be gone from this lawless town soon. There was no reason to concern himself over her anymore.

He picked up the prisoner's gun, then shoved it under his belt. With the prisoner firmly in his grasp, he made his way toward the jail. Once inside, he waited for the sheriff to secure the offender in one of the cells while he sat down and caught his breath.

The sheriff returned with two cups of hot coffee in his hands and passed Aaron one. "Thought you might need some. Your face is going to be sore. That felon gave you quite a punch."

Aaron rubbed his jaw and nodded. "I need to go and clean up, but before I go there is one thing you can help me with, Sheriff."

"Of course." The sheriff ripped the wanted poster off the wall and dropped it onto his desk. "The citizens of this town owe you our deepest gratitude, not to mention a hundred dollars in reward money for the capture of this Sean Roberts. What is it that I can do for you?"

Aaron leaned forward and decided to get right to the point. "Verified reports have been recovered that point to the fact that the gold stolen from the Union army is located in this area. I was sent to find it."

"Whoa, slow down." The sheriff shook his head as he slid into his chair. "You're not the first person to come charging into town with some grandiose idea that they are going to find the government's gold in these here parts and walk away with some hefty reward money."

"This isn't about the reward money. The government wants back what was stolen from them."

The sheriff tapped his pencil against the desk. "You probably won't believe this, but you're the second person today to walk in and tell me that they have information on where to find the gold."

Aaron sat up straight in his chair. "Who?"

"Another dreamer who thinks they can find fame and fortune by digging up some rumored pot of gold at the end of the rainbow." The sheriff's belly jiggled as he laughed. "I sent 'em to the land agent's office on another wild goose chase."

"What's his name?"

The sheriff shook his head. "Oh no. I shouldn't have even given you that much information. I thought it was bad enough to have one busybody poking around my town. Can't you see? This rumor has been circulating for years, and there's never been a sliver of proof that the gold even exists."

Aaron slapped his hands against the desk. "But I told you, I have documented sources who claim —"

"Who's making the claims, and what does that really mean? That someone's grandmother's cousin's uncle thought he saw a chest of gold being transported across his farm back during the war? Things like this don't just vanish. If there really was a trunk of the government's gold lying around, you can be sure that it's been spent by now." The man took off his glasses and held them up. "Now that I think of it, there's a man in

Des Moines who recently built himself quite a house. It's rumored to have ten bedrooms, seven fireplaces, and an entire wing for the servants. Of course, I ain't never seen it, so I can't say for sure. Maybe you should rush over there and see if he knows anything about the gold."

Ten minutes later, Aaron unlocked the door to his hotel room and slipped inside the cramped space. He didn't particularly like the sheriff, but he was glad for the tidbit of information he'd managed to procure from him. He might not have gotten a name, but one thing was certain. After cleaning up, he was going to pay a visit to the land agent, and find out just exactly who was after his gold.

# FIVE

Tara's head throbbed as she hurried down the boardwalk, leaving behind the embarrassing scene where she'd managed not only to slice her finger open, ruining one of her brand-new gloves, but also to faint dead away like some swooning female. When she'd come to, she'd managed to catch a glimpse of the sheriff and her lawman escorting the felon toward the jail.

*Her lawman?*

Her stomach tensed. The very thought was ridiculous. While she was relieved that the man had not been shot and killed, he wasn't hers — nor did she want him. Not that she could have him or had any intentions of going after him, because, undoubtedly, he felt the same way. He hadn't even come looking for her to make sure she was all right. No, the man had much better things to do than rescue her every time she managed to find herself in yet another embarrassing quandary.

Tara picked up her pace, determined to put an end to her rambling thoughts of a man she didn't even know. She was here for one reason and one reason only. To follow her aunt's leads and track down the government's gold. Period. No handsome strangers, no thoughts of love and romance. Too much was at stake.

Passing the barbershop, she noted that, once again, the street was filled with shoppers and businessmen carrying out their affairs as if nothing out of the ordinary had happened on this particular sunny July day. There were, in fact, no signs of the life-and-death situation that had, only moments before, given rise to panic in a number of the townspeople — herself included.

She passed a group of young girls, all wearing similar calico-print dresses and broad straw hats to block the summer sun. They eyed her curiously as they strolled by. Tara frowned and smoothed the front of her dress. Certainly, she looked a bit rumpled after scooting along the floor of the post office, where shards of glass had scattered across the dusty flooring. Ignoring the gaping stares, she pulled her bag closer and held her head high.

On the other hand, perhaps their curiosity had more to do with the fact that her dress, with its duchesse lace at the sleeves and silk edging, offered a peek at the very latest style from back east. Something one certainly wouldn't find in this part of the country.

A mother and child stepped out of the dry goods store in front of her. The child gave her a broad grin and waved before pointing at Tara and giggling. Suddenly, Tara wasn't so sure that the stares and gawking had anything to do with her tastes in fashion. The mother quickly whisked the young girl past Tara and toward the mercantile.

Tara frowned and put a hand to her head, wondering what could be so bad that . . . A hot blush scorched her face as she quickly pulled off the Stetson that still perched on her head.

How she'd managed to make such an obvious social blunder she had no idea. Tara glanced around, but everyone else seemed more concerned with his or her business at hand than the fact that she'd actually donned a man's hat in town. And a black Stetson at that. She felt her own hat to make certain it was still in place, then let out a deep breath as she continued on at a brisk pace for the land office. After taking care of her business there, she'd have to stop by the hotel and leave the offending article with Mrs. Meddler, assuming that was where the man was staying.

A bell jingled in the doorway of the land agent's office as Tara stepped inside.

"Can I help you, miss?" A tall, thin man with spectacles and curly tufts of blond hair poking out above his ears appeared from behind a tall stack of ledgers.

She held the black Stetson behind her back and smiled. "I'm interested in a particular piece of land, and wondered if you could possibly help me."

"Name's Horst Lehrer. At your service, ma'am." The man held out a bony hand and shook hers with more force than she expected.

"I'm Tara Young."

"If you're looking to buy a piece of property, Miss Young, then you've come to the right place."

Tara shook her head. "Actually, I'm looking for a piece of land that once belonged to a Mr. Richart Schlosser. From what I understand, he doesn't live in the area anymore, but I need to know which farm he owned. Possibly during the time of the War Between the States?"

"Mr. Schlosser. I recognize that name." The man rested his forefinger against his chin. "Give me just one moment. My wife says I have a memory that rivals that of anyone in the state when it comes to names. Never forget a name, no siree. Never forget a name."

The man began digging through the piles of ledgers while Tara stood patiently. Hopefully, there was some truth to the man's claims at never forgetting a name, but it was going to take more than a good memory to sort through the jumble of papers in this office. The odds of actually finding information on Mr. Schlosser seemed, well . . . she had her doubts such a miracle was even possible.

"Schlosser . . . S . . . Richart . . ." He picked up another ledger. "Let's see. Schlosser. It's a German name. Did you know that?"

"Interesting." Tara forced a smile. "I didn't know that."

"I like names." He glanced up at her. "And you're right, they are interesting. Take, for instance, my name. My last name is Lehrer, and it's German, as well. Means my father's grandfather, or perhaps his grandfather's father, was a teacher. That's where surnames originally come from, you know. Occupations, where one stays, or perhaps some unique physical characteristic. And my first name, Horst, means a thick grove. Always found that fascinating."

"I suppose, but —"

"My wife and I are expecting our first child in three months' time." He moved on to another stack of ledgers and flipped through the unorganized pile. "Having a tough time, though, trying to agree on the child's name. I want to pay close attention to the meaning behind the name, while my wife only cares about how the name sounds. You agree, don't you? That the meaning behind a name is just as important as the actual name."

Tara sneezed at the particles of dust that filled the room. "I . . . I suppose, though I can't say that I ever thought about it."

He pointed his hand at her. "Now, Tara. That's a lovely name. Do you know what it means —"

"I'm sorry, but I don't." She held up her gloved hand. "What about Mr. Schlosser?"

"Yes . . . yes . . . just one more place to look . . . Yes! Here it is. Mr. Richart Schlosser." He pulled a dusty file from the bottom of the stack and plopped it on the table in front of her.

A cloud of dust enveloped the stack of paper.

Tara sneezed again. "What does it say?"

"It looks to me as if Mr. Schlosser moved away after the war in sixty-six. Sold it to a man by the name of . . ." Mr. Lehrer turned his head to the right and squinted. "I can't quite read the writing."

Tara tapped her foot. "Who took notes on the transaction?"

"I did, but unfortunately my handwriting isn't nearly as clear as my memory."

Tara fiddled with the rim of the Stetson behind her back and prayed that he would come up with some sort of lead for her to follow up on.

"Yes, yes, now it's clear." Mr. Lehrer beamed. "It looks as if Mr. James Martin now owns that piece of land. Isn't far out, either. I'd say no more than five miles out of town to the west. You shouldn't have any trouble finding it. Now Jim isn't always the most hospitable man, but hopefully he'll know something about the whereabouts of Mr. Schlosser."

"So you have no idea what happened to the man?"

The land agent shook his head. "I remember the transaction between the two men. Met right here in my office to sign the deed papers. Mr. Schlosser seemed to be in a hurry to get out of town."

"What else can you remember? Anything

that might have seemed insignificant at the time might prove important to finding him."

He shrugged a shoulder. "I'm sorry, but that was four years ago, and I've had a lot of people go through this office."

"But your memory for names . . . details."

"Names." Mr. Lehrer shot her a weak grin. "Mr. Martin might know something. They appeared to be friends, though I can't say that for sure. I know that Mr. Schlosser planned to include the majority of his furniture in the sale of the property."

"Is that a common thing to do?"

"Happens from time to time. All depends on the circumstances, I'd say."

Tara gripped the back of a wooden chair with her hand. "So that's all you remember?"

"I'm afraid so, but if you're interested in a nice piece of land —"

"Thank you very much, Mr. Lehrer. You've been a big help."

Tara strolled into the bright afternoon sunlight, glad to be out of the dusty office, and hurried to the hotel. She hoped to find Mrs. Meddler before returning to the Carpenters' farm. While the woman's attire had been rather plain and, frankly, out of date, the lobby of the hotel exhibited a bit more taste with its warm terra-cotta walls and walnut furniture. Not that it could begin to compare with Boston's Parker House or any of the other luxurious East Coast hotels, but for someone needing a place to stay overnight, it would surely be a welcome sight.

Much to Tara's relief, Mrs. Meddler sat behind the front desk of the empty lobby reading a dime novel with its recognizable orange cover.

"Why, Miss Young." The older woman greeted her with a broad smile. "I was hoping you'd stop by for a cup of tea. I've been wanting to know how you were faring in your new place."

"It's good to see you, as well, Mrs. Meddler." Tara set the Stetson on the counter, debating what she should do. "And while I greatly appreciate the invitation, I ought to get back to the Carpenters. They sent me to town with a letter to mail after lunch, and I'm afraid I've taken advantage of their time. What I really need —"

"Nonsense. There's always time for tea." Mrs. Meddler snapped the book shut and hopped down from the wooden stool. "Don't tell my husband I'm reading this. I keep my stack of dime novels hidden away, because he's always telling me what a waste of time and money they are."

"Don't worry. My lips are sealed." Tara echoed the jolly woman's laugh, realizing just how nice it was to see a familiar face even if she barely knew the woman.

Mrs. Meddler shoved her book beneath the counter and waved her hand. "Come. You must stay for tea. We have so much to talk about, such as the shootout this afternoon. Were you in town at the time?"

"Yes." Hat in hand, Tara followed her into the large, airy kitchen where Mrs. Meddler began filling the kettle with water.

The older woman placed her hands against her heart. "Such a fright that gave me. I hid behind the front desk until my husband assured me it was once again safe to come out. What is this world coming to is my question."

"I have to agree." Tara leaned against a wooden cupboard and shuddered. "I was in the post office and found the whole experience quite terrifying."

Mrs. Meddler set the kettle on the stove and motioned for Tara to sit at a small table in the corner of the room. "Then trust me when I say that a cup of tea will help soothe both our nerves. Most appropriate, if you ask me. It will be ready in just a minute."

Tara placed the hat on a table covered with a white lace cloth, then made herself comfortable in the padded chair. Mrs. Meddler was right. She needed some time to recover from the ordeal. She took in a deep breath and made herself relax. Her stomach growled as her senses filled with the fragrant scent of meat and spices mingling with rising yeast bread.

"Perhaps I need to stay until dinner." Tara laughed. "Whatever you're preparing smells wonderful."

Mrs. Meddler pulled a sugar jar from the cupboard, as well as a small container of cream. "It's my own mother's recipe for gumbo. She was French and lived in New Orleans for most of her life. Believe it or not, it tastes even better than it smells."

Tara's mouth watered, and she couldn't help but wonder if she'd be offered yet another jar of pickles tonight.

Mrs. Meddler set two floral-patterned china cups on a tray. "Isn't Mrs. Carpenter a decent cook?"

Tara cocked her head. "Yes, though I have a feeling that I will have eaten my share of homemade pickles before I leave."

"Every social, picnic, and holiday isn't complete without a jar of Mrs. Carpenter's infamous pickles." Mrs. Meddler placed her hands on her hips and chuckled. "But don't you worry. Most of us have found various ways to avoid actually eating them."

"Then I suppose I'm going to have to get creative on this one."

Mrs. Meddler picked up the black Stetson. "Whose hat is this, by the way? You seem far too stylish to don one of these with your outfit."

Tara noticed the older woman's wink and laughed. "That's why I stopped by. You see, I'm not sure whose it is. A man left it behind at the post office during the shootout, and all I know about him is that he just arrived in town last night. He's tall with dark hair —"

"I know exactly who you are referring to." Mrs. Meddler spun the hat with a wide grin on her face. "Tall, solidly built with eyes the color of —"

"Toffee?" Tara felt a warm blush cover her cheeks. Something that was beginning to occur far too frequently.

"Exactly." Mrs. Meddler placed the hat back down and hurried to take the whistling kettle off the stove. "If I wasn't married, I'd consider snatching him up myself. Such a gentleman he is, too."

Tara giggled. "So you'll give him the hat, then. I don't even know his name."

"At a slight disadvantage then, aren't you?" Mrs. Meddler folded her hands across her chest and shook her head. "His name is Mr. Jefferson. Aaron Jefferson."

"Aaron Jefferson," Tara repeated.

"Now, have some tea. And who knows, perhaps Mr. Jefferson will come downstairs while you're here, and I can make the proper introductions."

Aaron opened his eyes with a start. Sunlight shone through the small window of his hotel room, casting a golden glow across the worn bedspread. He'd have to hurry if he was going to make it to the land agent's office before it closed.

His joints complained as he sat up. His own father had died when he was thirty-five, a seemingly ancient age for a boy of six. Now thirty-five didn't seem near as old as he'd once thought, but even though he still felt young at heart, that didn't mean he was as agile as he used to be. Slamming a ruffian into the mud and getting swiped across the jaw wasn't something he wanted to do for a living anymore. A gunshot in the shoulder two years ago had cured him of that. This latest assignment was supposed to be straightforward detective work. Not a stint in capturing criminals in the streets.

Aaron searched for his Stetson, then remembered he'd lost it at some point.

Maybe *she* had found it and had left it with the postmaster in case he stopped by looking for it. Feelings of guilt rushed over him. He should have gone back and made sure she was all right. The sheriff hadn't really needed his help escorting the prisoner to the jail, and their conversation could have waited.

*You're a coward when it comes to women, Aaron Jefferson.*

Shaking his head, he locked his room and headed downstairs. How could he have spent half his life fighting crime, taking down criminals, and risking everything to make this country a better place to live, yet become tongue-tied when standing next to a beautiful woman?

When standing next to *her*.

There was something about this particular blue-eyed woman with the auburn hair that left him feeling like an inadequate greenhorn instead of seasoned lawman. He couldn't help it. Her soft voice . . . the sincerity in her eyes . . . the way she smiled at him . . . had him completely captivated. Part of him hoped he ran into her again before he left town, while the other part of him preferred to finish his work as quickly as he could and avoid any such encounter

He headed outside, pausing only to nod

his greetings at the young woman working the front desk.

"Mr. Jefferson?

Aaron stopped near the entrance to the hotel. "Yes?"

"Is this yours?"

Aaron retraced his steps across the carpet, this time stopping at the desk where he picked up his Stetson. "Where did you find it?"

"Mrs. Meddler had wanted to give it to you herself, but she went to help with the delivery of Mrs. Acker's new baby. Anyway, before she left she said that a woman brought it by who thought you might be staying here."

Aaron fiddled with the brim. The faint scent of roses mingled with his own shaving soap. *She* had brought it by.

He had to know who she was. "Do you know the name of the woman?"

"No. Mrs. Meddler just said to be sure to give you the hat and tell you that the woman's name was . . ." The young woman's smile faded. "Perhaps she did tell me the lady's name, but . . . I can't remember."

"Was she young or old —"

"All I know for sure is that Mrs. Meddler said that a woman brought it by. I never saw her." She shrugged and turned back to her magazine. "Sorry."

"Thanks, anyway." Aaron set the hat on his head and started outside.

He was disappointed that he'd been so close to finding out who she was, just to come up against another brick wall. He'd have to speak to Mrs. Meddler once she returned. He shook his head. Whoever this woman was, she'd become a distraction. And he couldn't afford that. The government was counting on him to find the money. Which brought him back to his real concern.

Aaron crossed the street and headed toward the land agent's office. Truth was, rumors were always plentiful, especially when a large amount of money was involved. He had no doubt that there would always be others looking for the lost gold, but this person seemed to have information that was keeping him a step ahead. How could this person potentially know more than he did?

Unless the person had somehow uncovered specific information leading to the location of the missing gold.

# Six

Aaron glanced down the street, looking for the woman who'd delivered his hat. It had to have been her. Who else would have known where to find him? It appeared that she'd done a bit of detective work herself — but not a difficult assumption considering he was new to town and would most likely be staying at the hotel.

He tipped his hat at an older woman coming out of the mercantile and smiled in passing. Truth was, if he wanted to, he could do the same kind of investigation. In a small town like Browning City, it would be easy to find out where the Carpenters lived and, in turn, learn where she was staying.

Aaron pressed his hand against his front pocket and felt the crinkling letter of introduction signed by the chief himself. In his chosen career, when lives often hung in the balance, duty had to come before pleasure. In turn, thoughts of love and a family kept getting put off until after the next assignment came along.

*Or until I prove I can live up to my own family's expectations for me.*

Aaron pushed aside the thought and quickened his steps. This wasn't about his family. He simply didn't need the distraction from his work, especially when he had competition. The government would prefer not to pay the hefty reward money, but that could only be done if he found the gold first. And they were counting on him to do just that.

He stepped into the land agent's office and held back a sneeze. A layer of dust covered a desk piled high with papers and ledger books. The only two chairs in the small office were also covered with stacks of papers. He couldn't imagine how anyone could work in such an environment. Even the windows appeared as if they hadn't been cleaned for months, with their accumulation of grime from outside.

"Good afternoon. I'm Mr. Lehrer." A thin man appeared from the back of the room, held out his hand, and offered a broad smile. "How can I be of service to you today?"

"Name's Aaron Jefferson and I need some information." Aaron decided to get right to the point. "The sheriff said he sent someone to see you as they were tracking down either a person or perhaps the owner of a piece of land?"

The man shoved his wire spectacles up the bridge of his nose. "Today certainly is turning out to be quite a busy day for information."

"So someone did stop by?"

"About an hour or so ago. I answered a few questions, and we had a nice chat."

Aaron worked to conceal his interest. Finding this man might not be the ticket to finding the gold, but he wasn't going to ignore any leads.

"I need to know exactly what this person wanted."

Mr. Lehrer sat down at his desk and took out a steel nib pen as he shook his head. "I am sorry, but all transactions are private. You have to understand —"

"Not when it comes to the law." Andrew withdrew his badge from the front pocket of his vest and held it where Mr. Lehrer could see it.

Mr. Lehrer dropped his pen. "Who exactly are you?"

"I work for the United States government." Aaron shoved the badge back into his pocket. "I need to contact the person who was in here asking questions. He has some information I need."

"She —"

"She?" Aaron dipped his head. "I was under the impression that it was a man."

"Then you obviously haven't seen this woman. She was beautiful. Wide eyes, smooth skin, hair pinned up neatly, smartly dressed . . ."

An image of *her* filled his mind at the description. Aaron closed his eyes and tried unsuccessfully to push away the vision of the lovely stranger. The whole thing was ridiculous. How could he have become so enamored of someone he'd never properly met? He knew as much about Mr. Lehrer as he did about the woman. He had to forget her. Time to focus on this lead, not on a woman he very well might never see again.

"What else about her description?" Aaron leaned against the side of the desk. "What color was her hair?"

The land agent held up his pen and winced. "That, I'm afraid, I can't tell you. I'm color-blind."

"You're color-blind?" Aaron let out a sigh. All he needed were a few details, and he couldn't even get those. "Certainly you can tell me what she was looking for."

"Of course." Mr. Lehrer nodded. "A man by the name of Richart Schlosser."

Aaron worked to keep his frustration in check. In an office this unorganized, he wasn't sure he could trust the man's memory. "Are you sure that was the name?"

"I'm quite sure. I might be color-blind, but I never forget a name."

"And what did you tell her?"

Mr. Lehrer tapped his pen against the desk. "The man moved away about four years ago. James Martin now owns the farm."

Aaron stood up straight and tapped his Stetson against the palm of his hand. There was only one more thing he needed to know before he left. "Last question. What was the woman's name?"

"Her name is Tara Young. And if you're looking to find her, she was pretty persistent. I wouldn't be surprised if she heads out to Mr. Martin's the first chance she gets."

Tara finished reading aloud the last few verses from Psalms, chapter nineteen, then paused to take a peek at Mrs. Carpenter. The older woman sat sound asleep in her slat-back rocker. Tara yawned and wondered if she could sneak a few minutes of sleep, as well. Getting up at five thirty for the second day in a row, followed by boiling a new batch of brine for the pickles, had her longing for the quiet mornings back home where no one ever wakened her until the decent hour of eight or nine. And pickles were something they purchased from the shelves of the local grocer, never sweated over in the kitchen.

Her gaze rested once again on the weathered Bible with its thin pages. Her father had often read to her from the Psalms and other books of the Bible, but she didn't remember this particular one and its pronouncement that the Word of God was far more precious than gold. An interesting comparison, considering her own quest. While the thought was convicting, and she believed it to be true, her desire to track down the missing government gold had only intensified. Surely God would overlook her search for earthly treasures if He knew that her motives were in the right place.

How she was going to find the gold, though, was proving to be more difficult than she'd first imagined. Even now, she debated whether or not she should borrow the wagon this morning and pay a call on Mr. Martin. Not only did she worry about shirking her duties with the Carpenters, but obviously, a single woman such as herself paying a visit to a man she didn't know would never be considered appropriate. She wondered what Aunt Rachel would have done. There had to be a way to achieve her objective without tarnishing her reputation.

She pulled her copy of *Harper's Bazaar* out from under the edge of the serpentine-back sofa, determined to work on a plan as she flipped through the pages. While she'd read the magazine from cover to cover at least a dozen times on the trip here, she never tired of looking at the latest fashions. Skirts of pink coral trimmed with matching flounces and pink roses for the hair. Fawn colored silk parasol, and a gorgeous lilac silk walking suit with a violet tunic.

Tara turned another page, stopping at a drawing of a beautiful parlor set made of black walnut and a contrasting trim. She read through the description of the grand room with its bold Chinese red walls. Included in the drawing was an Italian inlaid table with matching mirror, heavy curtains, and even a sidewall arrangement of shelves where daguerreotypes and prints were elegantly displayed.

She eyed the Carpenters' old-fashioned sitting room with its worn fabrics and out-of-date furnishings and wondered if Mrs.

Carpenter would be opposed to a few minor alterations of the room. A bit of paint, stylish fabric, and rearranging of the furniture would do wonders for the room's mood. And it would certainly beat the pickling process.

Tara looked up at the sound of Mr. Carpenter's booted footsteps on the wooden floor. He stopped at the doorway and nodded in the direction of his wife. "She often falls asleep this time of morning if she didn't rest well at night, but she couldn't wait for you to read to her. Like mine, her eyes aren't strong anymore, and she has been missing her daily devotionals from the Word of God."

"I'm glad she enjoyed it."

Tara smiled, surprised at the feeling of contentment that washed over her. Though not quite as laborious as making pickles, reading aloud wasn't her favorite pastime. Knowing Mrs. Carpenter enjoyed hearing her read from the Bible shed a different light on things. While Tara had come to enjoy her years of education, it hadn't given her the chance to feel as though she were making a difference in anyone's life. And she liked the feeling.

"Why don't you go take a rest yourself?" Mr. Carpenter picked up a newspaper from his rocker and folded it under his arm before leaving the room. "You must be tired. With the pickles soaking and lunch simmering on the stove, I don't suppose there is anything else for you to do right now."

"I'm fine, really. I thought I would just read a bit."

He paused in the doorway. "It's a shame for you to have to stay cooped up inside. It's such a lovely day, but after your experience in town yesterday, me and the missus are a bit concerned about your safety. Granted, such a barrage of gunfire isn't a common occurrence, but all the same . . ."

Tara flicked at the edges of the magazine as his voice trailed off. If she could convince Mr. Carpenter to accompany her, she wouldn't have to worry about her reputation or her safety.

She cleared her throat. "While I understand your apprehension, I would love to go for a ride. I've always enjoyed exploring, and I wouldn't go far."

Mr. Carpenter pressed his lips together. "I just hate the idea of you out alone, but . . ."

Tara held her breath. A quick trip to town was one thing, barring another episode with a crazed gunman. Exploring the surrounding isolated farmland was different, and she knew it.

He tapped the newspaper against the wall. "I wouldn't mind at all going with you, though we'd have to take the wagon. I'm not much for riding horseback these days."

Tara glanced at his sleeping wife, remembering her words of caution, and wondered if she'd spoken out of turn. "I thought the wagon and your joints —"

"Don't you worry about me. The missus does enough of that. And besides, I need to get out of the house every now and then. Keeps me young."

Tara laughed. "Then I'll fetch my shawl and parasol and meet you outside."

Fifteen minutes later, they made their way up a grassy ridge. From this vantage point on the buckboard, Tara could see the surrounding landscape with its groves of oak trees and wildflowers nestled between cornfields that stretched as far as the eye could see. Sampson waved at them from the edge of one of the fields, his ever-present smile in place.

She waved back, then twirled her silk parasol between her fingers. "I hadn't expected Iowa to be so beautiful."

Mr. Carpenter nodded. "I agree with you now, but when Ginny and I first arrived, I wasn't sure I'd stay. Life was harder back then."

"Tell me about it."

Mr. Carpenter pulled back on the reins and slowed the horses to an easy trot. "The surroundings were quite different from what we were used to back east. Timber was limited, so we had to find alternative materials for building our homes and for fuel and fencing. We used things like Osage orange hedges for fencing, and our first house was made of sod. And there were other concerns. Not only did we have to build our own homes and our furniture, we also had to watch for signs of fires that could wipe out everything we'd built. It was lonely, and sickness was prevalent."

A frown covered the older man's normally jovial expression. Tara pushed a strand of her hair out of her face, struck by the hard life this couple had faced. "What made you decide to stay?"

"Besides being too stubborn to admit defeat?" Mr. Carpenter shook his head and laughed. "Things eventually began to change. The soil is rich and fertile, and as the population grew, we found ourselves connected to people again."

Tara couldn't help but notice the irony in the situation. "While you were longing for contact with people, we often complain that the city is too full of people."

"That, my dear, is one of the main reasons I left." Mr. Carpenter stopped at the top of another rise, showing her the beauty of the prairie that extended for miles. "Any place in particular you'd like to go?"

"Yes, actually." Tara paused, wondering how she should broach the subject. She didn't want Mr. Carpenter to find out about her search for the gold, but she needed his help to find Mr. Martin's farm. "I've been reading my aunt's journal, and she mentions a man by the name of Richart Schlosser. Did you know him?"

"Schlosser." Mr. Carpenter shook his head. "Can't say that I do, though that doesn't mean much. The railroad has brought scores of immigrants who have settled into the area."

"I found out in town that Mr. Schlosser moved away about four years ago, and James Martin bought his farm."

"Now there's a name I recognize. Lost his wife last year and hasn't ever been quite the same."

Tara leaned forward. "Do you know where he lives?"

Mr. Carpenter's eyes twinkled. "It's not far from here, if you'd like to stop by, though the man isn't extremely friendly."

"It's worth a try, if you don't mind."

With Mr. Carpenter's entertaining spin on stories from his past, it didn't take long before they reached the farmhouse that, at one time, must have been lovely. Wind, rain, and neglect, though, seemed to have worn away most of the character of the saltbox house. She wasn't even sure anyone still lived there.

Mr. Carpenter stopped the wagon in front of the house and called out, but his voice was quickly carried off by the wind.

Tara strained to look through the small glass panes in the front of the house, wondering if she should get down from the wagon and knock on the front door. "It looks empty to me."

The golden ball of the sun rose toward its zenith behind the farmhouse, leaving behind a trail of white light that pierced through the cloudy sky. The silhouette of a man on horseback appeared from the east and made its way toward the wagon.

She sat up straight and tried to block the sun with her hand so she could see the rider. "Is that him?"

"Could be, but I'm not sure. As I recall, Mr. Martin's rather small in stature."

Tall figure, broad shoulders, black Stetson . . . Tara's eyes widened as the figure came into view. Surely it wasn't Mr. Jefferson himself. She felt a blush cover her cheeks. She'd spent far too much time daydreaming about a man she knew nothing about, and now her heart raced at the mere thought of him.

The man on horseback bridged the gap between them, and a few moments later, she knew it was him.

"That's him," she whispered, grasping the seat to steady herself.

Mr. Carpenter gave her a sideways glance. "Who?"

"The man who rescued me at the station."

Aaron felt a surge of unwelcome anticipation run through him as he approached the wagon near the farmhouse. It couldn't be her . . . but it was.

He dismounted from his horse and tipped his hat. "I see we meet again."

Clear blue eyes stared back at him, and he wondered if she felt the same unexplained emotions he was experiencing. Today she wore a yellow dress and a straw hat that looked striking on her, but he couldn't remove his gaze from her face. Fair skin, rosy cheeks with perhaps a hint of a blush, long dark lashes . . .

She pressed her gloved fingers to her lips before responding. "We . . . Mr. Carpenter and I were just out for a morning ride."

Remembering his manners, Aaron turned and nodded at the older gentleman. "It's nice to see you again, sir. This young lady and I have met twice in rather unusual circumstances yet have never been properly introduced."

"And I am afraid that I have the advantage." She closed her parasol and set it in her lap, while he waited for her response with great interest. "Mrs. Meddler from the hotel told me your name when I left your hat."

She smiled at him, and he feared his heart might burst from his chest.

He cleared his throat. "Which, by the way, was very kind of you. I'm glad to see, as well, that you are all right after that frightening incident in town yesterday. I apologize for not returning to find you, but I needed to help the sheriff —"

"Please don't worry about me." She shook her head. "I was a bit shaken after the episode, naturally, but I have recovered completely from the incident."

"I am very glad to hear that."

Mr. Carpenter coughed beside her. "No wonder the two of you have never introduced yourselves. How could you when you spend your entire time exchanging such sugary pleasantries?"

Aaron caught the surprised look on her face before turning to Mr. Carpenter. A look that no doubt mirrored his own. Surely his attraction toward the woman wasn't that apparent.

Mr. Carpenter gave them both a toothless grin. "Mr. Jefferson, I'd like to introduce you to my cousin's granddaughter, Miss Tara Young."

# SEVEN

Aaron automatically reached out to shake her hand while his mind fought to make the connection. "I'm very happy to make your acquaintance, Miss Young."

*Tara Young?*

Aaron felt the muscles in his jaw tense. Surely he had misunderstood the elderly gentleman.

He caught her gaze. "It is Miss Young, isn't it?"

She pulled back her hand. "Yes. Why do you ask?"

Aaron frowned. This couldn't be Tara Young, fortune hunter and gold digger. This woman was too beautiful and cultured to have traveled to Iowa simply to track down the government's lost gold. It just didn't make any sense.

"Is something the matter?" Her eyes darkened, seemingly as unsure at his reaction as he was by the news he'd just been handed.

"Of course not, it's just that —"

"You'll come back to the farm for lunch now, won't you, lad?" Mr. Carpenter saved Aaron from having to come up with a response. "It's the least we can do for your having saved Miss Young's life."

"Twice." A smile lit up her face, causing his pulse to hammer.

Aaron forced a smile in return. He had no desire to deceive her, but the only way he was going to find out her source of information was to learn what he could about her. There was no time like the present to follow this unexpected lead, and he'd just been given the perfect opportunity. It also didn't hurt that the woman of his current inquiry happened to be beautiful and engaging. A far more interesting task than the majority of his assignments.

"Lunch would be nice. Thank you." Aaron nodded and followed beside the wagon at a slow pace.

He also wouldn't mind a home-cooked meal. Not that the meals at the hotel under the watchful eye of Mrs. Meddler hadn't been acceptable, but nothing surpassed a real home-cooked meal.

Aaron rested his hands on the leather pommel and let the rhythmic motion of the saddle take away some of the tension that had formed in his shoulder muscles. "Do you know the owner of this farmhouse? I'm assuming you had planned to pay a visit on the proprietor."

She flashed him a coy smile. "I admit I thought the same about you. Strange we would happen to visit the same farmhouse on the same day. It's too bad no one was home."

"It is quite a coincidence, isn't it?" Aaron adjusted the brim of his Stetson, wondering how to explain why he was here if asked directly.

Miss Young swatted at an insect buzzing around her head. "I was intending to speak to the owner. A Mr. James Martin. Do you know him?"

"No, but I was hoping to meet him. Why did you need to speak to him?"

"It's a bit of an involved story, since I've never actually met the man." She leaned back against the buckboard and let the parasol block the sun from her face. "My aunt knew the previous owner of this land, and I was hoping Mr. Martin might know where he lived now. I'd like to find the man."

"A close friend of your aunt's, I assume then?"

"They were . . . acquaintances."

He watched out of the corner of his eye as she pressed her lips together. Obviously the woman had some secrets to hide. He turned his attention to the horizon as they headed west toward the Carpenter farm. She didn't trust him. Yet. And rightly so, because he was a complete stranger. The fact he carried a badge might help, but he needed something more. Something that would help shed light into his character of being one who was both sympathetic and trustworthy. Not simply a tough, rugged lawman.

"And what about you, Mr. Jefferson?" She eyed him skeptically. "Why did you need to see Mr. Martin this morning?"

"I'm considering buying a farm in the area." The words tumbled out before Aaron had considered the consequences.

Her eyes widened. "This land's for sale?"

"I'm not sure about this farm, to be honest." Aaron stumbled over his words, wishing he could erase his previous statement.

The muscles in his back tensed. Something happened to him when he was around this woman, and now he'd gone from tongue-tied to sharing private matters better left unsaid.

He offered her a weak smile. "I know there are several farms for sale in the area, and

I've found in life that it never hurts to ask."

"You're certainly right, young man." Mr. Carpenter flicked the reins to pick up the horse's pace and nodded. "Martin's property would need a lot of work, but you have a good eye for land. Fertile soil with a number of streams going through it. I've often thought it a pity that this piece of land has been neglected for the past few years."

Miss Young cocked her head. "Still, I must say that I'm surprised because I had assumed that you were from back east and only here temporarily. Somehow as a lawman you don't seem the type to settle down and run a farm."

"It's true that I've lived most of my life in the saddle, traveling from place to place, but . . ."

Aaron dug the heels of his boots into the sides of the mare. He was managing to dig himself a hole, and if he wasn't careful, he'd end up burying himself alive. He hadn't planned to talk about his plans for the future. These were dreams he hadn't intended to share with anyone.

He cleared his throat. "My grandparents moved to Iowa in the forties, and I lived about fifty miles from here until I was twelve."

While he rarely allowed himself to dwell

on the idea, he had always dreamed of buying his own piece of land along the Mississippi River, or perhaps a large farm in the middle of the state. He would raise cattle and hogs and watch the corn grow.

He drew in a deep breath and savored the familiar smells of the land. The sweet aroma of wild roses mingled with the earthy scent of the fertile ground. Somehow she'd managed to remind him how much he loved the land. Along with a John Deere plow, he'd form straight furrows in the dirt that would then nourish the seeds of a crop.

Not that he didn't enjoy what he did. He'd spent his entire life working hard to get ahead and live up to his family name. His grandparents and his parents had passed away years ago, but that didn't change the fact that being a lawman was in his blood, and there was nothing he found more satisfying than bringing an outlaw to justice, and, in turn, making the country a safer place.

For seven months now, he'd stayed in hotels night after night while chasing down leads for the government on a cache of gold that many believed didn't even exist. From Washington DC through Virginia and a corner of Pennsylvania, he'd followed every piece of information his superiors had passed down to him. But these days, he was tired of traveling. He was tired of being alone.

He glanced at Miss Young with her frilly dress and silk parasol. She belonged in an elegant parlor back east, not riding on a decrepit wagon across the endless Iowa prairie. Which brought back to mind the question as to why she was here. It was time to find a way to move the focus of the conversation from himself to her. Not only did he need to avoid starting any rumors about why he was here, he needed to find out everything she knew.

He cleared his throat. "So what really brought you to Iowa, Miss Young?"

Tara swatted at a mosquito and paused before answering the question. From the resolute expression on Mr. Jefferson's face, she was certain there was something more to his inquiry than simply a way to fill the minutes until they arrived at the Carpenter farm. A few moments ago, she would have assumed that he had posed his question in order to get to know her better. She'd seen the look of interest in his eyes the first time they met at the station, then again outside the post office when his hand had brushed across hers, causing shivers to run up her spine. And she was certain he'd felt it, as well.

Something, though, had changed. She'd felt it the moment Mr. Carpenter introduced her and said her name. Though he tried to hide it, the surprise on Mr. Jefferson's face had been clear. But why? Perhaps she was only fearful about someone finding out why she was here. Rumors regarding the gold had circulated for years, but she was certain the information she held could easily start a stampede across the state if she wasn't careful.

But he couldn't know why she was really here. Her conversation with the sheriff had been made in the strictest of confidences. While she wasn't so naive to believe that he might not share the information she'd given him with another lawman, what reason did the sheriff have to even mention the gold? He'd told her himself that searching for the gold was a ridiculous waste of time, and she had no reason to doubt he believed that.

She'd also been careful when speaking with the land agent, cautioning him never to mention the gold. Even Mr. Carpenter had no reason to suspect why she had come to Iowa. So what was it?

She looked down at her attire and frowned. The yellow crepe dress with its overskirt of the same fabric wasn't exactly an appropriate choice for a ride through the cornfields. Wide ribbon sashes and lace edgings were more suited for an afternoon visit to one of her parents' neighbors. She fiddled with the silk trim of her sleeve. She couldn't help it. The very thought of wearing a simple calico garment made her skin crawl.

Tara stared at the soft fabric until her eyes crossed. Perhaps Mr. Jefferson, like her own parents, didn't believe she belonged on a farm, living in the middle of Iowa. And perhaps they were right. But wasn't that exactly what she had set out to prove? If she failed to go ahead with her quest, she'd never know if she was capable of more than speaking a few witty phrases of conversation at a party and looking pretty.

"Miss Young? Are you all right?"

Tara looked up at Mr. Jefferson, surprised that the farm was already in view. She nodded. "Of course. I'm sorry. I suppose your question made me think about home."

"Do you miss Boston?"

"Not as much as I thought I would." She didn't want her answer to sound shallow. "Even with its conveniences, the city is dirty, noisy, and overcrowded. Still, I miss my friends, the architecture, artwork, and even the church we attend every Sunday."

"To ease a bit of your concern, Pastor Reeves's preaching can rival what any big city has to offer," Mr. Carpenter said reassuringly. "He's a man of God who preaches straight from the Word."

"I'm sure you're right. I just . . ."

Tara's voice trailed. Mr. Jefferson looked at her as they approached the farmhouse, and her pulse started to race. She turned away, determined to find a way to discover the gold while at the same time keeping her heart intact.

# EIGHT

Aaron crunched down on another pickle and smiled. It had been a long time since he'd sat at a family table and shared a meal, albeit one with such an interesting family, to say the least. Mr. Carpenter, with his denim overalls and toothless grin, was proving to have an unlimited reservoir of comical tales from his adventurous past. He sat at the end of the table and kept them entertained with story after story while Mrs. Carpenter, when she wasn't bustling around and making sure everyone had what they needed, sat beside him, listening as though she were hearing the narratives for the first time.

Aaron's gaze turned to Miss Young, something he'd found himself doing far too often during the meal. She sat forward slightly, her eyes wide with interest, and her food seemingly forgotten as she listened to the story Mr. Carpenter told of a cattle stampede that almost killed him when he worked as a cowhand in his younger days. While she looked somewhat out of place with her fancy dress and impeccable manners against the worn furnishings of the dining room, one thing was notable. She didn't seem to possess the arrogant attitudes he'd observed in most young women of means. Such a realization was refreshing.

Not that her manners and propriety mattered to him, because they didn't. Not in the least. And just because she happened to be both beautiful and modest was no cause for him to get distracted from the real reason he was here. His duty was to find out what information Miss Young had regarding the gold. Starting with, perhaps, the obvious question as to why a woman of noticeable means had traveled across several states to work as the caregiver for two elderly relatives. Were the Carpenters a key to finding the gold? Or did Miss Young's information lay solely with her aunt's acquaintance, Mr. Schlosser?

No matter how many times he tried to convince himself that he was only sitting at the Carpenters' table and eating stew and sour pickles because he needed to learn why she was here, he found himself lost in her smile and the soft lilt of her laugh. Aaron frowned. Perhaps it was too bad that she wasn't homely. It would certainly have made the job easier for him and given him fewer distractions to face.

Seemingly unaware of the effect she had on him, Miss Young pushed back an unruly curl that had fallen across her cheek. "So what made you leave the life of a cowboy, Mr. Carpenter?"

The older man squeezed his wife's hand. "I met this beauty and decided there was more to life than earning a living in a saddle."

Aaron took a bite of stew. Looking at the older couple, he realized that all their years of marriage hadn't faded the love between them. He couldn't help but wonder if he'd ever be so blessed to find a woman willing to share a life with him through whatever the future held.

He frowned again. Since when did he allow thoughts of love and marriage to run so rampant through his thoughts? He'd settle down one day and buy that farm, facts he'd impetuously shared with Miss Young, but there were other things that had to be done first. He gripped the edges of his chair and, for the moment, couldn't remember any of his excuses . . . couldn't remember why he shouldn't let his heart lead the way for once in his life.

He finished off his pickle, determined to change the subject. "When did you settle in Iowa, Mr. Carpenter?"

"Eighteen thirty-six. Seems like yesterday in so many ways."

"My husband is right. I still remember those first few years when all we could do was try to survive." Mrs. Carpenter passed Aaron the bowl of pickles and laughed. "Didn't even have a good cucumber patch back then. Which reminds me. You mustn't let me forget to send you home with a jar or two of my pickles, young man."

Aaron smiled and took another one. If making a good impression meant eating yet another sour pickle, he was happy to do it. There was a lull in the conversation as they finished the thick stew and homemade bread. It seemed the perfect opportunity to ask about the gold without anyone perceiving his real intentions. Who knew better what had happened in this territory the past few decades than Mr. Carpenter? And if the man had information . . . Aaron decided to take a chance.

He buttered a slice of bread. "You've lived in this state for a good many years, Mr. Carpenter. I've heard rumors that the government lost a cache of gold in these parts. Have you ever heard such a claim?"

While Aaron addressed Mr. Carpenter, he watched Miss Young out of the corner of his eye. He saw the flicker of something in her expression as her brow lowered. Surprise? Worry?

Mr. Carpenter waved his hand in the air, shaking his head. "Son, there've been rumors of gold in this country for as long as I can remember, from lost gold to gold mines. Look at Illinois and Georgia back in the twenties, California in the forties, Colorado, Nevada . . . why not Iowa? If you ask me, the rumors are usually nothing more than a bunch of nonsense."

"I suppose you do have a point." Aaron set his spoon down and wondered if the man could be right.

It wasn't a new thought. The government had supplied him with confirmation that the gold still existed. He'd interviewed dozens of sources from Washington DC to the banks of the Mississippi, and many of them had led him a step further, but to what? To the truth that the gold was nothing more than a rumor? His superiors denied such a charge, but after months of searching, there were times when even he was beginning to doubt. No gold meant that everything he'd invested in this assignment had been for nothing. And that, in his mind, was unacceptable.

"If one looks closely at history, there are always very few men who actually make it rich in the gold runs." Mr. Carpenter held up his spoon. "The Good Book tells us that the Lord and His decrees are far more precious than gold. It's a shame a few more people don't believe that. The world might be a better place if we did."

Aaron nodded his head. "Another good point, sir."

But the Good Book also said, "Whatsoever ye do, do it heartily, as to the Lord, and not unto men." Which was exactly what he was trying to do. And if his quest ended up proving nothing one way or the other? Did his hard work make up for his failure in God's eyes?

Mr. Carpenter wiped his face with his napkin, then scooted back the chair. "Miss Young has yet to have seen much of the beauty of this area, including the stream that runs through the edge of our property. Perhaps the two of you would enjoy a bit of exercise. It's lovely this time of year."

Aaron shook off the dismal questions that troubled him, and instead, looked at Miss Young and tried to read her expression. There was nothing he'd rather do at the moment than spend the afternoon with her, and he'd just been given the perfect opportunity.

He pushed his plate away. "Miss Young, I believe I could spare an hour or so if you'd enjoy a short ride."

He was certain he saw a tint of blush color her cheeks before she responded. "That would be nice, Mr. Jefferson, but I need to first clear the table and wash the dishes."

"Nonsense." Mrs. Carpenter stood and took a plate out of Miss Young's hands. "You already worked half the morning on my pickles. I'd say you deserve a bit of time for yourself."

Miss Young rose to protest. "But —"

"Just enjoy yourselves. I'll let you prepare dinner once you return."

Tara rode beside Mr. Jefferson on one of Mr. Carpenter's horses as they made their way toward the creek east of the property. From the rise in the terrain, she could see the far bank of the stream that flowed through the edge of the Carpenters' property. Yellow rays of afternoon sun hit the clear water, leaving behind tiny diamonds that danced in the ripples. Beyond the stream, instead of cornfields, lay acres of tall prairie grass, yet to be plowed.

Mr. Carpenter was right. It was a perfect day for riding, and the landscape, as she'd already come to discover, was beautiful. Only she could hardly concentrate on the view with Mr. Jefferson riding beside her. They'd discussed a number of intriguing political topics from President Grant's recent defeat against the Senate in his attempt to annex the Dominican Republic to the appointment of the first black to congress.

She stole a peek at the handsome lawman. Their discussions had soon moved to a spiritual thread, but as much as she enjoyed their conversation, she realized she still didn't know what had brought him to Browning City. Vivid images of adventure and romance filled her mind, like something out of one of Mrs. Meddler's dime novels. Maybe he was on the trail of a notorious desperado, or perhaps an entire gang of outlaws. Surely the fact that he'd saved her twice ranked fairly insignificant against the dashing heroics he'd accomplished in his career.

Mr. Jefferson turned and noticed her gaze. She dipped her head, embarrassed he'd caught her staring at him. The knowledge that she was blushing again infuriated her. She'd spent her entire life learning how to be a proper lady who strove to be dignified and elegant at all times. Why, then, did one look at Mr. Jefferson melt every sense of decorum she could muster and leave her feeling vulnerable and defenseless?

He cleared his throat. "May I be so bold as to ask you a question?"

"I suppose." She adjusted the fabric of her russet colored riding costume against the coat of her dappled mare.

Mr. Jefferson's eyes had turned a pale shade of caramel in the sunlight. "I'm curious as to why a beautiful and cultured young woman, such as yourself, chose to come to Iowa. From your dress and manners, I'm assuming you don't need the income."

Tara frowned.

"I'm sorry, if my question is at all offensive —"

"No, it's just that . . ." That what?

She played with the brim of her wide straw hat, wanting to believe that his question was not a barb intended to prick her conscience. But what if he saw her as a shallow individual looking for a bit of adventure at the expense of an elderly couple's generosity? Or even worse, being a man of the law, he might wonder if she had lost her financial position and was only here to prey on the financial assets of her remaining family.

Before arriving in Iowa, she'd never stopped to consider the fact that her attire would be out of place amongst the rolling hills of Iowa. But what was she to do? Toss her stylish wardrobe in exchange for a closet filled with hand-sewn clothes made from gingham fabric from the mercantile? She'd always taken pride in her appearance, but here it seemed to be a constant disadvantage rather than an asset.

Tara pulled back on the reins to slow the mare as the bank of the creek appeared before them. She wondered what she should say. She certainly couldn't mention the gold, but not stating her real reason for coming might prove just as suspicious.

"While I've only been here a short while, I believe the arrangements with my distant relatives is working out well. They needed someone to help around the house, read to them from the Bible and such, and I wanted to see a bit more of this part of the country." She didn't give him time to respond before posing her own question. "What about you? Besides the fact that you are a lawman, I know little about why you are here."

She watched as he pressed his lips together and turned his head slightly. It seemed that she wasn't the only one with a secret. Of course, being a lawman, he had the right, she supposed, to keep his mission undisclosed, but that didn't squelch her sense of curiosity.

He clicked his tongue and pulled the horse to a stop before dismounting. "I'm doing some work for the government. Most of it is confidential, though, I'm afraid."

And undoubtedly important.

Suddenly her dreams seemed very shallow and insignificant. How was chasing down a rumored pot of gold any better than pursuing clothes, fashion, and parties back east? Not that her entire life had been full of such shallow objectives. A good portion of her time had been spent in charity work. Her small offerings, though, never seemed enough to make a difference in anyone's life. The poor continued to funnel into the church for food twice a week, and the children in the orphanage always needed new clothes and shoes. There never seemed to be enough time or resources to meet all the needs.

Searching for the gold had been a way for her to do something important. Her one chance to do something beyond the mundane tasks of everyday life. But her quest to aid the government seemed insignificant. Her parents had saved dozens, if not hundreds, of lives by being a part of the Underground Railroad during the war. She'd seen glimpses of wide-eyed children with their ebony skin as they scurried with their parents into the cellar below the house. The same heroics had been true for her aunt Rachel. Slipping messages to key people had made a small yet significant difference in the outcome of the war.

What good was ladling soup into the bowls of the poor twice a week when those same individuals would go hungry the next night? It wasn't a solution; it was simply postponing the inevitable. And what good was a pair of shoes to a small child who needed the love of a mother and father?

"Can I help you down?" He stood beside her horse with a ready hand to aid her.

Tara pushed aside the unwelcome thoughts and swallowed hard at his nearness. "Please."

She felt the strength in his arms when he lifted her off the horse as if she were no heavier than a sack of goose feathers. Not wanting to meet his gaze, she studied the tip of his chin and its small dimple. Once her feet hit the ground, she couldn't stop herself from looking up briefly and smiling to thank him.

His Stetson blocked the sun that had

begun its descent into the western sky. Everything around her faded, and for a moment, she couldn't breathe. No longer could she hear the song of the goldfinch, or smell the scent of the wildflowers blowing in the soft summer breeze. It was just the two of them and a strange connection she couldn't explain. Her horse stamped and nudged her in the back. She clasped her hands and turned away, breaking the suspended moment.

Aaron took a step back. Something had passed between them, but he wasn't sure what. All he knew was that there had been something in her eyes as she'd looked at him that had reached all the way to the depths of his heart. It was something unexpected, something he couldn't explain. And he didn't know if he wanted to.

He reached down and picked up a couple of smooth pebbles. There was too much at stake. His superiors were beginning to pressure him. Finding the gold was not only a governmental priority, his career hung in the balance, as well. He had no time for distractions. And he needed to find out what she knew.

He walked toward the stream edge and skipped a stone across the glassy water. He wouldn't lie to her, but telling her the truth would no doubt push her away. It would turn him into the opponent instead of a potential suitor. Not that he had any chances of actually becoming her suitor.

"There is something I need to tell you." He tossed another pebble into the creek and watched it skip across the water.

Miss Young leaned against the trunk of a tall tree beside him with a lazy smile across her face. He wondered what would happen if he bridged the distance between them and kissed her. He shook his head and pushed away the ridiculous thought. Confronting her might be the last thing he wanted to do, but it was what he had to do.

He stared at the water flowing slowly toward the south. "I know why you're here."

"Excuse me?"

"I know that you're not really here to take care of the Carpenters." He turned to face her. "I know about the gold."

She took a step forward and raised her chin. "The gold?"

"Gold stolen from the US government at the end of the war. That's why you're here. To find it."

"How did you . . . ? I don't understand."

Aaron clasped his hands behind his back. "It's a small town, Miss Young. One really

121

can't trust anyone to keep a secret, especially when it comes to gold."

"Sheriff Morton." She shook her head and looked up at him. "So what do you want from me?"

He scuffed the toe of his boot against the ground, wishing things could have been different between them. "I want you to give me the information you have and stop looking for the gold. I will pay you for any tip you give me that leads to the finding of the cache."

"You can't be serious." Any feelings of attraction that had glimmered in her eyes a few moments ago were gone. "Why should I do that?"

"Because I'm a lawman who's qualified to track down the information and who's working for the government."

"I don't see how your qualifications have gotten you anywhere so far." She shoved her fists against her hips and frowned. "Otherwise, you wouldn't still be chasing down the rumored gold or trying to extract information from me."

Aaron felt the veins in his neck pulse. "I'm not —"

"And let me tell you something, Mr. Jefferson." Her fists balled at her sides. "I have no intention of telling you, or anyone else, the information I have. Do you think I left the comforts of my home in Boston to come to this place and simply give up?"

He shook his head. "You don't understand what's at stake here — or the danger your life could be in if the wrong people get involved."

"No, I don't think you understand." Miss Young crossed the grassy knoll to where they had tethered the horses and attempted to mount the mare.

He hurried to her side to help her, but she held up her hand to stop him. "Thank you, but I don't need your help, Mr. Jefferson. Not now. Not ever. I have proof that the gold exists. Mark my words. It's only a matter of time before I find it."

# NINE

*Tara swallowed hard and forced her horse to sprint faster. She could feel her heart pounding in her chest, but she refused to give in to fear. Fear was the enemy, and time was running out. It had taken two weeks, but she'd finally managed to unravel the majority of the clues in her aunt's journal. She'd also discovered that there were others searching for the gold. Others who would do anything to get their hands on the journal she possessed.*

*But that was something she'd never allow.*

*The house loomed before her in the distance. The shabby saltbox structure her aunt had written of was the key to the gold. That she knew for sure. All she needed was to unlock the last few paragraphs and her service to her country would be complete. If her assumptions were correct, she'd be able to secure the gold before the others.*

"The masked bullion my comrade holds, remains forever secluded beneath the ring of woody perennials, there to be confined until the adversary is trounced."

*She repeated aloud the phrase from the journal. Masked meant hidden. Bullion referred to the gold. My comrade —*

*A gunshot ripped through the morning air. She slid to the ground, bringing the horse to an abrupt halt. Then she clutched the journal beneath her arm as she ran to the side of the house for cover. Another shot pierced the morning stillness. The enemy had arrived before her. She caught sight of his black Stetson as he rounded the corner, and her breath caught in her throat.*

*It wasn't the adversary from Aunt Rachel's journal.*

*It was Mr. Jefferson.*

Tara sat up with a start, then lay back down too quickly, whacking her head against the headboard. A rooster crowed outside. The sun had yet to wrap its warm fingers across the acres of farmland and prairies, but already she could hear Mrs. Carpenter bustling downstairs. In a few moments, she'd knock on Tara's door and announce the start of yet another day.

Tara let out a long sigh. For two weeks now, she'd risen before dawn. Today, she wanted to sleep in. Between morning Bible readings, farm chores, and evening prayers, they'd spent the time cleaning every nook and cranny of the house, an undertaking Tara was convinced hadn't transpired for at least half a decade. And while she hadn't been able to talk Mrs. Carpenter into making any major changes in the antiquated furnishings, she had to admit that she was amazed at the transformation that had occurred.

Mrs. Carpenter continued to sing her praises, claiming that she'd never have had the energy to accomplish such a feat without Tara's help. But for a city girl who'd never placed one foot on a farm before arriving in Iowa, the housework hadn't been the only challenge. From milking the cows to collecting the eggs to ensuring the new lambs didn't escape from their pen, she'd fallen into bed exhausted at night. Even the last of the pickles had been sealed in mason jars yesterday afternoon and lined up in neat rows in the cellar until the next church social. And all of this had given her little time to pursue the gold.

Tara reached over and lit the kerosene lamp beside her bed before pulling out her aunt's journal from beneath her pillow. Stifling a yawn, she opened the pages to the one she'd marked. Aunt Rachel's handwriting was easy to read, but the meaning behind it was often coded. In her dreams the meaning seemed clear, but in real life the answers were far less easy to interpret. She was sure she was missing something important in her aunt's writings, but exactly what, she didn't know.

One thing was certain, however. Mr. Jefferson was not mentioned in her aunt's journal. But that didn't stop him from plaguing her dreams. She'd seen him twice since his insistence that she stop her search. Both times had been at church, which wasn't a setting where she could openly speak her mind. So, instead, like any proper lady, she'd made sure that she was well mannered and cordial as she greeted him. But that was it. She refused to be taken in by his enchanting eyes or his smile that set her heart to racing, not once forgetting that he had become her opponent.

She pulled her robe closer around her shoulders. She hadn't forgotten Pastor Reeves's words, either. His convicting sermon from the book of Colossians had lingered with her, reminding her that she wasn't to serve men, but God. And once again, her motives for coming to Iowa came into question. Trying to please others while proving she could do something valuable with her life perhaps wasn't as noble as she'd once thought.

Shoving aside feelings of guilt, Tara fingered the edge of the journal and read once again the entry for April 17, 1864.

"Received word from MS today. Further contact unsafe."

Tara squeezed her eyes shut, wishing her aunt Rachel were here to explain the words she'd penned. Tara missed her so much. But crying certainly wouldn't accomplish anything. From an earlier entry, she knew that MS stood for Mr. Schlosser, and that he had been one of her aunt's contacts. Aunt Rachel herself had once confided some of the secret code that had been used and had told her that the bullion referred to the government's gold. But secured where?

She needed to speak to Mr. Schlosser. Mr. Martin, her only connection to Mr. Schlosser, had been away for the past month and was planning to return today. Somehow, in the middle of laundering the bedding and washing the feathers from the mattresses and whatever else Mrs. Carpenter had planned, she was determined to slip out of the house and find a way to pay a call on the man.

She'd made several friends in town, including Constance Van de Kieft and the pastor's wife, Mary, but telling the Carpenters she was going visiting at one place while actually calling on Mr. Martin wasn't an option. Neither was taking Mr. Carpenter with her this time. The older man was feeling somewhat under the weather, and Mrs. Carpenter was insisting he stayed at home until he felt better.

Tara quickly changed her clothes. Then she tugged on the bottom of her short cape with determination. She would just have to take a chance and go by herself, and hopefully, she'd be able to find answers to her questions.

She opened the door to Mrs. Carpenter's cheery grin. "Good morning, Miss Young. I was just about to knock. You're up bright and early."

Tara forced a smile, feeling anything but chipper at the older woman's greeting. "Good morning, Mrs. Carpenter."

"I've brought you something more suitable to wear."

Tara's brows rose in question as she took the calico garment that was thrust into her hands. For the past few weeks, she'd donned two of her own simpler dresses while working. Neither was fit to wear in public anymore, but they'd been suitable for the work they had done.

Tara held up the plain dress that had to

have been made decades earlier. "What am I to do with this?"

"I wanted to surprise you." Mrs. Carpenter held up a worn cookbook.

Tara frowned. A calico dress, a dog-eared cookbook . . . and a surprise? Something worse than making pickles? Tara wasn't sure she was ready for one of Mrs. Carpenter's surprises.

The older woman hugged the book to her chest. "I've been wanting to make a wool sweater for Mr. Carpenter, and thought what better time now that you are here. You can help me with the dye bath and the spinning —"

"Excuse me, Mrs. Carpenter." Tara held up her hand in protest. "I have never spun wool let alone dyed wool —"

"You mustn't worry." She shot Tara a broad smile. "I'm going to teach you."

Tara set the gallon pot full of the used dye bath on one of the porch steps, then headed toward the clothesline with the wool. After a morning of washing and rinsing the wool, then making a dye bath and coloring the wool, she was ready to crawl back into bed. Still, she had to admit that the rich plum color of the yarn would make a stunning sweater. If she only knew how to make such an item — which she didn't.

Of course, that was bound to change. Mrs. Carpenter planned to teach her not only the dyeing process of the wool that she'd learned today, but also the spinning and actual crafting of the garment. While she could embroider and do other simple forms of needlework, such a task was not something she'd ever attempted. Nor had wanted to. That was the very reason she enjoyed the ease of readymade fashions from the city where she could purchase the costumes featured in *Harper's Bazaar* with little effort.

While Mrs. Carpenter went to start lunch, Tara had simple instructions to hang the dyed wool out to dry in the shade before fetching a few potatoes from the cellar. She was hoping that as soon as lunch was over, she'd be able to pay Mr. Martin a visit.

One of the lambs bleated behind her, and Tara spun around to shoo the young animal back into its pen. How it managed to escape from the confines of its enclosure she had no idea, but it wasn't the first time she'd had to chase the little animal back to its mother.

"Now, Cotton Ball." She placed her hands on her hips and spoke sternly to the lamb. "I don't have time for any nonsense today. I've got to finish up here so I can go and

131

meet with Mr. Martin." She leaned down to whisper the last sentence. "He's going to help me find the gold."

Cotton Ball skittered to the right. Tara lunged for the lamb and missed. He went to the left, and she followed his move, before he made a quick maneuver toward the house . . . and the tub of dye.

"No . . . no . . . no." Tara's eyes widened in horror. "The dye is for after you've been sheared, not before . . ."

She picked up her skirts and ran after the lamb. All she needed was a plum colored lamb in the sheep pen. What would Mr. and Mrs. Carpenter say to that? The lamb continued toward the tub at a brisk pace with Tara right behind. If she could stop the lamb before it tried to run up the stairs . . .

Tara didn't see the stump until it was too late. Tripping across the lawn, she fell flat on her face at the bottom of the staircase. Frightened by her scream, the lamb tried to run up the stairs and landed in the pot of dye.

Tara looked up in horror. The tub teetered on the edge of the stair while the lamb struggled to get its footing. Tara tried to get up, but she was too slow. Cotton Ball moved forward, and the entire contents of the tub, sheep and all, dumped on top of Tara's head.

Aaron stuffed the telegram into the pocket of his denim pants and frowned as he walked down the crowded boardwalk toward the livery. For two weeks now he'd followed every lead he had, and his superiors were not going to be pleased with his findings. His discrete conversations with three suspect people in the area, had, like the rest of his efforts, turned up no new leads. His opinion now was that there was no proof left the gold ever existed. And it if did, no doubt it had been broken up into smaller lots and spent years ago.

Now they wanted him back in Washington by the end of the month. With answers. One would think that the government, with its recent establishment of the Department of Justice and other political concerns, would be less inclined to worry about a cache of lost gold. But apparently that wasn't the case.

Wiping the sweat off the back of his neck with his hand, he longed for a tall glass of lemonade to quench his thirst from the hot and humid afternoon. Maybe when he returned from Mr. Martin's, he'd stop by the hotel restaurant. But because his superiors wanted answers, he was determined to follow through on the assignment until he found the gold — or until he uncovered solid evidence that the gold was gone.

He'd spent his entire life working to get ahead, trying to live up to the name his parents had bestowed on him, Aaron Thomas Jefferson, and to the high standards of his family lineage. This assignment was no different. He might not have forgotten his grandfather's spiritual nurturing, which tried to teach him to rely on Christ alone, but those words had faded as the years progressed and had been replaced by a determination to forge ahead on his own.

"Mr. Jefferson?"

Aaron stopped in front of the barbershop. He'd almost walked by Pastor Reeves without even seeing him. "It's good to see you again, Pastor."

The man stood before him with a few pieces of mail in his hand. "My wife wanted to invite you to supper, but you always slip out of church so quickly, we haven't had a chance to ask you."

"I'm sorry, sir." Aaron tipped the brim of his Stetson to block the sun. "I'm not planning to stay in town much longer, I'm afraid."

The friendly preacher laughed. "Hope it

isn't my sermons that are running you off."

Aaron couldn't help but like the man and his sense of humor. "Not at all. In fact, your lessons have been quite timely."

Enough to prick his conscience and to cause him to reevaluate his life and the motives behind what he did. The man had a point when he pressed that service to God had to come before trying to please man. It wasn't a thought he planned to brush off without some serious consideration.

Pastor Reeves tapped the mail against the palm of his hand, seemingly in no hurry to end their conversation. "I heard you were interested in buying a farm in the area. Does that mean you might return soon?"

"Buying a farm? I . . . I'm honestly not sure at this point."

Aaron frowned. Perhaps it was time to go back to Washington. There was no telling what other rumors regarding why he was here were circulating in this small town. News that he was searching for the gold was the last thing he needed right now. And if Miss Young had been involved —

"Either way, I hope to see you at church on Sunday." Pastor Reeves reached out to shake his hand. "And don't forget, you're more than welcome to stay for lunch afterward. My wife makes the best dumplings this side of the Mississippi."

Aaron forced a smile and shook the man's hand. "I appreciate your kindness, Pastor Reeves."

Aaron watched the man of God make his way toward the small church building that sat on the edge of town. While he honestly did value the man's kindness, thoughts of food, no matter how delicious, were low on his priorities right now as he strived to stay focused on the job at hand.

He'd even managed to forget about Miss Young. At least most of the time.

She, though, was the reason he was in such a hurry today. Rumor had it that Mr. Martin had arrived home late last night from a trip to see family members. And Aaron was determined to talk to Mr. Martin before Miss Young had a chance to show up and ruin everything.

Securing the feisty stallion he'd rented from the livery while he was in town, Aaron followed the road until Mr. Martin's worn saltbox house came into view. Little had changed since his first visit two weeks ago when he'd encountered not only an empty house, but had also learned the identity of Miss Young. He scanned the horizon and the unspoiled land, thankful there was no sign of the woman today. Luck must be on his side. Mr. Martin sat out on the front steps.

He stopped in front of the house and dismounted. "Mr. Martin? Name's Aaron Jefferson. I was wondering if I could speak to you for a moment."

"What do you want?" The balding man took a swig of whatever he was drinking.

"I won't take much of your time, but I'm trying to find out about the —"

Mr. Martin turned away at the squeaky wheel of an approaching wagon.

Aaron followed his gaze, his heart plummeting when he realized who was driving the wagon. "You've got to be kidding."

"Why? You know the woman?"

"Yes, in fact, I do." Aaron dipped his head to block the sun. Miss Tara Young sat erect in the wagon, heading straight for Mr. Martin's house. "It would seem as if you have quite a number of visitors today."

The man set his drink down and stood. "Strange. I'm not used to company."

"Mr. Martin, I really would like to speak to you, but would you excuse me for one moment, please?"

Mr. Martin shrugged. "Don't make any difference to me. I ain't going anywhere."

Aaron rushed across the dusty drive toward the wagon, determined to speak to her in private before she ruined any chance he might have at an interview with Mr. Martin. She pulled on the reins to stop the horses and eyed him skeptically without saying a word.

He folded his arms across his chest and let out a deep sigh. "Miss Young. It appears we meet again."

# TEN

Aaron opened his mouth, but everything he wanted to tell Miss Young vanished. Why was it that one look at her auburn hair and bright blue eyes left him completely enchanted to the point that he wanted to forget she was the opposition? He'd worked hard to erase her from his daydreams, but nighttime had been another story. She'd occupied his dreams, and seeing her again only reinforced the unpleasant truth that she'd completely captured his attention.

He shoved his thumbs in his belt loops. "I . . . I wasn't expecting to see you again."

Her cautious smile didn't reach her eyes. "We are after the same pot of gold, are we not?"

Aaron took a step closer to the wagon. Something wasn't quite right with her appearance. While she was impeccably dressed as always with her pink dress and matching parasol, something had changed. A jumble of curls was held neatly beneath a straw bonnet, but her hair seemed to be a shade or two darker. Almost a . . . a plum color? And her fair cheeks had splotches of purple. If she'd come down with something . . .

"Are you feeling all right, Miss Young?"

She fiddled with the ribbons that held her bonnet in place beneath her chin and looked away. "Of course I'm all right. Why do you ask?"

Aaron cocked his head, wondering if it would be better to simply drop the subject, but curiosity got the better of him. "Your face is a bit —"

"Purple?" She looked him straight in the eye. "Then may I suggest that you should never fall into a dye bath, especially one that has been made with very potent berries? It tends to stain the skin temporarily. Or at least it did to me, and I assume that explanation will satisfy your curiosity regarding the slight change in my appearance."

He pressed his lips together and suppressed a laugh. He should have never brought up the issue, but now that she had acknowledged something had happened, he had to know more. The subsequent images she'd invoked were far too amusing. "You fell into a dye bath?"

"It was the lamb, actually, but that doesn't matter." She held up her hand as if to stop him from asking any more questions. "Mr. Jefferson, may we please return to the topic at hand?"

He paused. "The topic at hand?"

"Mr. Martin and the gold. I'm assuming that you are here for that reason."

"But the lamb —"

"The gold, Mr. Jefferson."

"You're quite right. And Mr. Martin's connection." Aaron eyed a small spot near her chin that he imagined to be in the shape of a heart and cleared his throat. She must have been in quite a hurry to beat him here to have failed to remedy her appearance. "I know I cannot force you to leave, but I want to make it clear that I will be the one who will conduct this interview."

She held her head high. "I suppose you believe that would be to my advantage, considering you are the one qualified in the areas of investigations and interviews."

"I . . . well . . . Of course I am." Aaron shook his head. She was doing it again. Here he was in a professional capacity, and she was leaving him tongue-tied. He needed this lead and couldn't afford for her to ruin it for him.

Miss Young picked up her parasol and

held out her hand. "Would you mind helping me down, Mr. Jefferson?"

Aaron paused. He didn't want to feel the softness of her gloved hand. He didn't want to wonder what it would be like to kiss her, or —

"Mr. Jefferson?"

"Of course. I'm sorry." He took a step forward and grasped her hand to help her descend, but he didn't let go after she'd stepped on the ground. "Do we have a deal, Miss Young?"

"That I remain silent during the interview?"

"Exactly."

She bit the edge of her bottom lip and didn't respond for a moment. Aaron's jaw tightened. He knew he had a fine line to walk. He needed Miss Young for this investigation more than she needed him. Mr. Martin might hold the key to finding Mr. Schlosser, but if Miss Young held further information that might lead to the discovery of the gold, he couldn't afford to make her angry. Winning her trust again might be the best method, but that didn't change the fact that he needed to be in charge of this investigation and, in particular, the interview with Mr. Martin. She might be able to charm her way into the lives of those involved, but he was the one experienced in the interviewing process.

"Knowing that you are a professional," she finally offered, "I will do my best not to interfere, but —"

"Miss Young." He wondered if his request for her to remain silent was possible. "I need more than an *I'll do my best* from you."

"Please do not worry. This is just as important to me as it is to you." She opened her parasol to block the sun. "But let me remind you that I was the one who secured this information for you in the first place. Without it, I believe, you are out of leads."

"I wouldn't go that far, Miss Young."

"We shall see, but for now, I think we have a job to do. Mr. Martin is waiting."

Tara followed Mr. Jefferson, willing her hands not to shake. She couldn't believe that she hadn't managed to beat the man here. If it hadn't been for the unfortunate incident with Cotton Ball and the dye . . . She let out a long sigh, determined to forget the fact that, in her rush to beat Mr. Jefferson to the farm, she'd failed to completely get rid of all the signs of the purple dye.

There was no telling what the man thought of her now, but she didn't care. Or at least she didn't want to care. All she needed to do was focus on getting the information she needed, regardless of the fact that *he* was walking beside her, close enough that she could smell the spicy scent of his shaving soap and see the solid form of his stature. She shook her head. She still held her aunt's diary, which meant she had the upper hand. A fact that Mr. Jefferson no doubt found extremely annoying.

They stopped in front of the porch, and Mr. Jefferson addressed the owner of the farmhouse. "I am sorry for the interruption."

Mr. Martin took off his hat and scratched his head. "You never told me why you were here, Mr. . . ."

"Mr. Jefferson. Aaron Jefferson." Aaron reached out to shake the man's hand.

"And my name is Miss Young." Tara stepped forward, determined not to be pushed aside by Mr. Jefferson. "We're here to find out some information regarding the man you bought this property from. A Mr. S—"

Tara felt the insistent jab of Mr. Jefferson elbow against her upper arm, then caught his piercing stare. She frowned. Keeping her word was not going to be easy.

Mr. Jefferson grasped her elbow. "Would you mind if we came in for a moment, Mr.

Martin? I promise we won't take up much of your time."

Mr. Martin rubbed his chin. "For a minute, I suppose."

Tara walked beside Mr. Jefferson up the stairs, trying to ignore the fact that his touch made her pulse race and forget why she was here. Distraction was the last thing she needed at this moment. Ignoring his presence, she instead took in the details of the weathered saltbox house. Inside, the sitting room was sparsely furnished with little more than a sofa, three chairs, and a table. Lace curtains, a shade of dull grey, hung on the wall, obviously not having been washed for some time. A handmade quilt lay on the back of the sofa, but its faded colors showed only a hint of what it once must have looked like with stunning reds, yellows, and purples. A daguerreotype of a woman sat on a small table beside the sofa, but beyond a few throw pillows and books, there were no other personal articles.

Mr. Martin motioned to the worn sofa, and Tara sat down beside Mr. Jefferson. "I'd offer you both something to drink, but I've just arrived home. Not much left in the pantry."

"Please, don't concern yourself." Tara set her parasol beside her, then folded her hands in her lap. "We didn't come to take advantage of your hospitality."

"Allow me get straight to the point, Mr. Martin." Mr. Jefferson sat forward and rested his elbows against his thighs. "We are looking for the previous owner of this house, a Mr. Schlosser. We were hoping you might know of his whereabouts."

"Mr. Schlosser? I have no idea." Mr. Martin sat down in the rocking chair and shook his head. "Ain't seen the man since I moved into this house a good four years ago."

Tara didn't try to stop the flood of disappointment that swept over her. Without Mr. Schlosser, unless she could interpret more of the journal on her own, she was out of leads with nothing further to go on. Which in turn meant she was no closer to finding the gold than Mr. Jefferson was, a thought that brought with it a large amount of frustration.

Not wanting to waste any more of the man's time, she rose to leave, but Mr. Jefferson motioned for her to sit back down before he spoke. "During the transaction, Mr. Schlosser must have given you some indication as to where he was going."

"Said he was headed west. Montana . . . South Dakota?" Mr. Martin shrugged a shoulder. "Can't say that I rightly remember. Besides, don't think the man ever stayed anywhere long enough to put down roots. He'd only lived here about two years when he up and sold the lot. Always wondered where he got his money. Never seemed to work much but traveled all the time."

"A traveling salesman perhaps?" Tara struggled to take deep breaths and slow her pulse. What if Mr. Schlosser had taken a part of the government's gold to fund his own undertakings? She had to know more.

"A salesman's got to have a product. And as I recall, there were no goods."

Mr. Jefferson wasn't finished. "We understand that when Mr. Schlosser sold you the property, you also bought all the furnishings."

Mr. Martin nodded. "I did, but if you look around you can see that none of it was worth much. Tables and chairs, the sofa, a bed, and an old chest were all he had to offer."

Tara's brows rose. She hadn't thought of that angle. Perhaps there was a spark of hope after all. What if Mr. Schlosser had left some of the letters behind in the chest? Some clue to the location of the gold that could be interpreted only by someone who knew him or her aunt Rachel . . . like herself.

Mr. Jefferson cleared his throat. "You mentioned a chest. Did there happen to be any papers inside?"

Mr. Martin rocked back in his chair, his eyes narrowing at the question. "Why exactly do you need to find Mr. Schlosser?"

Tara shot Mr. Jefferson a worried look, afraid they'd pushed the man too far. They arrived as complete strangers and were now asking him to make a search of his house for possible missing articles.

"My aunt —"

Mr. Jefferson whacked the heel of her shoe with the toe of his boot. She clenched her hands together. The man was without a doubt completely exasperating. Granted, she had to admit that he was quite good at extracting information, but that didn't mean that she had no right to participate in the interview at all. Surely she came across as less of a threat than the tall, rugged lawman beside her.

Mr. Jefferson avoided her gaze. "Miss Young's aunt knew Mr. Schlosser. They exchanged letters throughout the years, and as a sentimental gesture, Miss Young is trying to track them down."

"Mr. Schlosser wasn't married, but I —"

"They were only friends, but it's very important we track down these letters."

Mr. Martin rubbed the stubble on his chin, then rose from his chair. "I'll be right back."

Mr. Jefferson waited until Mr. Martin had disappeared down the hallway before speaking. "You're not doing a good job of keeping your part of the deal."

"I'm sorry, it's just that —"

"There's a lot at stake here, Miss Young."

"For both of us."

Tara picked up the daguerreotype beside her. Fighting with Mr. Jefferson wasn't the answer. What was it about him that made her want to scream with frustration while at the same time made her desire to know everything he was thinking? If it weren't for the missing gold that had managed to wedge its way between them and their opposing goals to find it, she would have liked for their relationship to turn in another direction altogether. She'd seen the interest in his eyes, despite the fact that he now saw her as the opponent and not a lady to call upon.

She took a peek at him, knowing he was praying right now that when Mr. Martin returned, he'd carry with him the answer to their search. His lips were pressed together, and his hands were clasped tightly in his lap. He was determined to track down this gold with or without her. And something told her that his resolve had a personal meaning to it. Perhaps they both were looking at things wrong. Unwavering from their quest as they sought to prove themselves. Or maybe he didn't have anything to prove. Maybe it was just a job to him.

She studied the photo of the young woman in her hand. While her dress was plain and she wasn't smiling, there was a softness in her expression.

Tara looked up as Mr. Martin stepped back into the room. "She's beautiful. Who is she?"

"Is that why you're here?" Mr. Martin's face reddened as he crossed the room in three long steps.

While he hadn't actually welcomed them warmly into his home, any signs of friendliness had vanished from his expression. He reached to grab the photo from her. The frame slipped out of her hands, and glass shattered against the floor.

"I'm sorry." Tara covered her mouth with her hand.

Mr. Jefferson stood. "Mr. Martin —"

"Now look what you've done." The man's eyes flashed as he glared at them. "Mr.

Schlosser was just an excuse, wasn't he? A reason for you to come into my home without my knowin' your true intentions."

Tara pressed her back against the sofa, feeling the rise of panic fill her stomach. "Of course not, but I —"

"My wife is none of your business." Mr. Martin pulled a rifle off the fireplace mantel and pointed it at them. "Now get out. Both of you. You've done enough damage for one day."

Mr. Jefferson grasped Tara's elbow and pulled her up from the couch. "Mr. Martin, I promise you, we had no intentions to —"

Mr. Martin fired a shot into the ceiling. Bits of dust filtered through the afternoon sunlight that streamed through the window. "I said, get out."

With Mr. Jefferson at her elbow, Tara tripped across the wooden floor, praying with each step that it wouldn't be her last.

# ELEVEN

Aaron kept his hand on Miss Young's elbow as they hurried down the wooden porch steps toward the wagon. How was it that he'd come to ask a few simple questions and ended up almost getting shot? He didn't know what there was about this woman, but she certainly seemed to be a target for trouble. The attack at the station, the incident at the post office, and now this . . . even her new violet shade of hair seemed to be a sign that the woman couldn't avoid getting herself into a mess. And with a sheep and a pot of dye bath no less.

Grabbing the reins of his horse in his free hand, he escorted them both across the hard ground outside Mr. Martin's house toward her wagon.

Miss Young bustled beside him to keep up. "Mr. Jefferson, I am sorry. I never intended —"

"If you would just be quiet for a moment,

please." Without stopping, Aaron turned to check on the whereabouts of Mr. Martin. The last thing he wanted was a bullet in his back.

The middle-aged man stood in the door-way watching them, but thankfully, he'd set the gun down beside him. Mr. Martin might not seem to be mentally stable, but that didn't change the fact that Miss Young's presence could have cost him not only a lead in his case but also his life. There was no telling how much more he might have uncovered on his own. Mr. Martin had gone to look for something, and now Aaron was quite certain that he'd never know what it was.

"It looks as if he's not going to shoot us." Aaron gritted his teeth. "Though I'd say that's the only good thing about this morning."

"I hate guns." Miss Young stumbled on the uneven ground, and he tightened his grip to steady her. "Mr. Jefferson, I said I was sorry. I thought my presence could help, my being a woman and all. One would think that he would prefer to open up and talk to me over a lawman like yourself."

"Your charm might do wonders at a church picnic, parties, and other social gatherings, but as you can see, it had little effect in a professional capacity." Aaron frowned. His words might hold a dash of truth, but hadn't she managed to work her way straight into his heart? "Besides, sorry won't change the fact that Mr. Martin will never want to speak to either of us again."

He stared out across the fertile pastureland toward the west, where a decent-sized herd of cattle grazed, and scowled. While his words held truth, he'd seen the compassion in her eyes as she'd asked Mr. Martin about the woman in the picture and heard the gentle way she'd talked to him. In truth, it wasn't her fault that the man got upset. But all of that didn't change the fact that they'd lost a valuable lead, and unless he wanted to take another chance at getting shot, he was going to have to come up with another way to find Mr. Schlosser.

Working on an alternative solution, Aaron stopped at the wagon to help her onto the buckboard. She lifted the hem of her skirt and pulled herself up into the wagon, ignoring his outstretched hand. He dropped his arms to his sides and grunted. He'd never met a more stubborn woman.

"I'm going to accompany you home." He scratched the back of his neck and wondered if he were simply a glutton for punishment as her blue eyes widened.

Tara picked up the reins and clicked her tongue at the horse. "I don't need an escort, Mr. Jefferson."

Aaron raised his brow as he mounted his horse. "Considering the fact that you can't seem to stay out of trouble, I believe an escort would be most appropriate."

She reached up to touch the back of her hair, and despite the seriousness of the situation, Aaron found himself wanting to laugh. The shade of purple was actually quite becoming on her. There was little doubt in his mind that life around Miss Young would never be dull.

Which was exactly what was bothering him. Aaron stared straight ahead as they left Mr. Martin's house and tried to avoid the temptation to sneak another peek at her. She was beautiful, intelligent, compassionate . . . why then couldn't she drop this ridiculous quest to find the gold?

And then what? Did he really think that would change things between them? That he would find a way to court her? He was leaving soon and would most likely never see her again. Even if he did buy a farm and settle down somewhere nearby, Miss Young wasn't the kind of woman who would be content living the rest of her days on a secluded farm in Iowa. He was quite certain that she wouldn't last six months here. Once the cold hit and the snow began to fall, she'd no doubt miss her upscale Boston home with its piped-in gas and plush furnishings. Besides that, Browning City boasted little shopping or parties or . . .

He looked at her and willed his heart to not to care. While her cheeks were rosy and her eyes bright, her jaw was set in determination. She was just as determined as he was to find the gold. But that wasn't all. The gold had just been an excuse as to why things wouldn't work between them. The truth was, even without the quest, they'd never be able to make a relationship work. They were simply too different. Their relationship would prove to be more difficult to achieve than finding the government's lost cache.

He would accompany her to the Carpenters' farm, then say his farewells. He still had a chance to find Mr. Schlosser — on his own. But first he owed her an apology.

He tipped the brim of his Stetson. "I'm truly sorry for my harsh words, Miss Young. While the situation was strained, you didn't deserve such a reprimand."

Tara's eyes widened at the apology. She had expected a lecture, not a confession from the man riding beside her. He was turning out to be quite an anomaly. Practiced law-man on one hand yet willing to ask for forgiveness when the situation warranted such an action. She found the gesture not only surprising but also refreshing.

"I do appreciate the apology, but . . ."

She hesitated. Apology or not, it was obvi-ous that his own determination to find the gold hadn't wavered. And she'd just lost her last lead. Until she could either interpret the rest of her aunt's journal or find Mr. Schlosser through another means, instead of returning home a hero, she was stuck in Iowa eating pickles, carding wool, and whatever other messy project Mrs. Carpen-ter asked her to do.

She looked to her right at the endless sea of corn planted by one of Mr. Martin's neighbors. At first, she'd found the setting monotonous, but she had to admit that there was something about the open space of the land and lush rolling hills that gave her a sense of peace she'd never felt before. She loved the sincerity of the people and the quiet surroundings after the constant rush of life in Boston. Even the fresh scent of the summer air was a welcome relief from the congestion of the city. But that didn't mean she wanted to stay.

Mr. Jefferson's plan to buy a farm had briefly caused her to entertain the idea of staying in Iowa. But it would be presumptuous to even imagine that he would ever want to share his piece of land with her. That he'd want to share his life with her.

"Were you going to say something?"

She glanced up at him as he spoke and bit her lip. He was handsome, intelligent, even compassionate at times. Why then couldn't he allow her to continue her quest to find the gold? In the end, both she and the government would be happy, albeit the government would be out the hefty reward money. No. She was determined not to let Mr. Jefferson's handsome profile and undeniable charm get in the way of her proving her worth to her family.

"It doesn't change anything, you know." She braced herself as the wagon went over a slight dip in the road.

"What doesn't change anything?"

"Your apology. While I do very much appreciate your kindness in the situation, I'm still determined to find the gold."

Mr. Jefferson's lips curled into a slight smile. "I hadn't expected anything less from you, Miss Young. I believe that in the past few weeks of our acquaintance, I've come to recognize that your determination matches your beauty."

"I . . ." She closed her jaw, now knowing what to say in response.

If he was trying to sweet-talk her, he was doing a fine job. But she wasn't going to let him manipulate the situation. His profile, tall and well built while sitting high on the back of a black stallion, was one that took her breath away. But she wouldn't allow such thoughts to fill her mind any longer. There was certainly more to life than good looks, and all the charm in the world wasn't going to remedy the situation between them. No, she would return to the Carpenters' home, do her best to manage all the jobs Mrs. Carpenter asked her to accomplish . . . and find the gold.

*The judgments of the Lord are true and righteous altogether. More to be desired than gold . . .*

The passage from Psalm nineteen fluttered through her mind. She gripped the reins tighter and frowned.

*But I don't actually want the gold, Lord. Just the . . .*

Just the what? The recognition? The chance to prove herself to her country in an important fashion? The honor that would come with finding something the government hadn't been able to track down for years? Something that even Mr. Jefferson hadn't been able to track down.

*Where your treasure is, My child, there will your heart be also.*

Tara rode in silence beside Mr. Jefferson, her heart suddenly heavy with the Lord's clear reminder from His Word. She couldn't deny the truth. She'd been so wrapped up in following the treasures of this earth that she'd stopped focusing on storing up treasures in heaven.

*Can't I do both, Lord?*

There had to be a way. The Carpenters' farmhouse came into view, and while she couldn't ignore the pointed words, neither was she ready to let go of her search.

*I need to do this, Lord.*

She was tired of living in the shadow of her parents and aunt. While there might be little she could ever hope to achieve in her life that would come close to their noble accomplishments, she'd never forgive herself if she didn't at least try. The last thing she wanted was to wake up one day, old and unhappy, because she'd failed to do something important with her life. Surely the good Lord understood how she felt.

Tara brought the wagon to a stop in the front yard. Clothes fluttered in the breeze on the clothesline. A sheep bleated in the pen, and she caught sight of the violet colored lamb. Turning away, she sighed. Good looks and charm had never proved to be enough. She'd always managed to bungle what was important.

She turned and caught Mr. Jefferson's gaze, hoping he hadn't noticed the tangible results of her morning escapades running through the sheep pen. "You know I'm going to do this on my own."

He shot her a grin. "And so am I."

"I wouldn't expect anything less from you."

*What does God expect?*

She tried to push aside the words, but they lingered in the back of her mind.

"Then may the best man, or woman as the case may be, win." Mr. Jefferson tipped his hat, then with the nudge of his boots against the side of the stallion, he raced across the fertile farmland and out of sight.

Aaron wanted to hit his head against the wall. He'd spent a week tracking down Mr. Schlosser, but every lead had come up empty. Except the last one. The rumors were plentiful, but the final piece of proof had just confirmed that Mr. Schlosser had died in a mineshaft somewhere in South Dakota eighteen months ago.

He glanced around the hotel restaurant that was empty except for an older couple sitting at a corner table. Sunlight streamed through windows that overlooked the main street of town. At least today, all seemed quiet as shoppers hurried about their business. With red tablecloths, a stone fireplace, and a few simple paintings, the atmosphere was as pleasant as the meal. But today he could barely taste the food.

He dropped the telegram onto the table and took another bite of the roast beef and potatoes he'd ordered for lunch, frustrated. Another dead end. And perhaps his last. There was only one thing left for him to do before returning to Washington with nothing more to show for his efforts than a handful of hotel bills.

He was going to have to speak to Miss Young. If he didn't, he would have to admit that he'd run this investigation as far as it would go, and it was over. He wasn't yet ready for that. Not when there was a chance for one last lead.

Aaron picked up the pencil and piece of paper he'd borrowed from Mrs. Meddler and began to scrawl out a message. It wasn't as if he didn't want to see Miss Young again. Because he did. Every day, as he walked the streets of town, he watched for her, but there had been no sign of the beauty. He'd even considered stopping by the Carpenters' farm, knowing the elderly couple would welcome a visit from him. But he hadn't. He was ashamed to think that his pride had gotten in the way of seeing her again, but there seemed little other explanation. Instead of that line of thought, he focused on the note he was writing.

Dear Miss Young,

I have new information and a proposition you might find interesting. Please meet me for coffee at the hotel restaurant tomorrow at two if it is possible.

Sincerely,
Aaron Jefferson

He tapped the pencil against the table. He wasn't sure his plan was going to work and that she'd actually agree to see him, but he didn't have much choice. Aaron reread the note one last time. A young boy who worked at the hotel walked into the restaurant, and Aaron called him over to his table. The boy had promised Aaron he'd deliver the message to Miss Young for a small fee. Aaron pulled out some change from his pocket and set it on the table beside the note.

It was time to call a truce.

## TWELVE

Tara fingered the note, surprised at Mr. Jefferson's desire to meet with her. Of course, the request was strictly business, but that didn't stop her pulse from quickening at the thought of seeing him again. For the past week, she had attempted to put him and his piercing toffee colored eyes out of her mind, but her efforts were in vain. He'd managed to leave an imprint on her heart that she couldn't erase. And no matter how irritated he made her with his determination to find the gold single-handedly, she hadn't been able to ignore his other, more gallant, characteristics. His apology, for one, had shattered any remaining impressions that he was simply a tough lawman compelled only by his assignment. The man had a heart.

She stuffed the request into the pocket of her apron, then finished drying the last of the dishes. With both new information and a proposition, she couldn't help but wonder exactly what it was that he had discovered. Her attempts to locate Mr. Schlosser had resulted in nothing. No one in town seemed to remember much about the man, and she didn't have the resources Mr. Jefferson had. With no leads to follow, she'd stayed up late at night reading her aunt's journal by the smoky light of a kerosene lamp, trying to uncover any additional clues that might lead to the gold. But the result had only left her frustrated — and tired.

Mrs. Carpenter bustled into the kitchen with two jars of pickles in her hands. "You've done a fine job, Tara. Thank you so much for your help. With my joints seemingly stiffer by the day, I don't know what I would do without you."

Tara smiled at the comment. For the first time in her life, she was finding satisfaction in hard work. "Are you sure you don't mind my going into town this afternoon?"

"Not at all, dear." Mrs. Carpenter set the pickles on the kitchen counter and dug through a drawer until she pulled out a thin red ribbon. "The fresh air will do you good. I told Mr. Carpenter last night that you've been working far too hard this past week. Between farm chores, the garden, and knitting, you've had little time for yourself."

Tara placed the stack of dry plates on the shelf, then wiped her hands on a towel. She was surprised at how much she was beginning to enjoy life on the farm. While the Carpenters had primarily retired and now rented out the majority of their land to tenant farmers, there was still plenty of work.

Certainly, she missed her mornings of sleeping in and never relished the early crow of the rooster, but she'd found a sense of pride in seeing the results of her efforts on the breakfast table or in a batch of jam to be given away to the tenants' wives. There had even been enough of the purple wool for her to start her own shawl. Something she'd never imagined herself doing.

Mrs. Carpenter tied the ribbon around one of the jars and made a neat bow. "Can I ask you to do a favor for me?"

"Of course."

"Dr. Harding's wife, Wilma, is a bit under the weather. If you wouldn't mind taking her one of these jars. My mother always believed good homegrown food to be good for the constitution, so I figure why not my pickles? And the other jar is for that handsome lawman, Mr. Jefferson."

Tara felt a blush creep up her cheeks at the mention of his name. "You know, of course, that our meeting is strictly for business. He has some information on an old friend of my aunt's that he wants to pass on to me."

Mrs. Carpenter rested her hands on her hips and smiled. "It's a shame he won't be stopping by the farmhouse. Feel free to invite the gentleman over for lunch. Perhaps Sunday after church, if he isn't too busy."

"I will." Tara slipped the yellow apron over her head and folded it.

Thoughts of church left her feeling somber. While her quest for the gold had uncovered few, if any, answers regarding its location, the pursuit had exposed a vast number of spiritual questions. And like the gold, the answers seemed out of reach.

She placed her apron on the counter, then tapped her fingers against the wood. "Mrs. Carpenter, would you mind if I asked you a question?"

The older woman worked to tie the second ribbon. "Of course not. I may not have all the solutions, but I do have a listening ear."

"Is it wrong to want to do something important?" Tara fiddled with the hemmed edge of the apron and tried to rework her question so she said what her heart really felt. "I guess what I'm trying to say is, is it wrong to want to something that perhaps would . . . would prove one's self to the world? To prove that one is . . ."

". . . Worth something?"

Tara winced. "That sounds shallow, but yes."

Wasn't that exactly what she was trying to do? Prove her worth to herself, her family, and even God?

Mrs. Carpenter cocked her head. "I suppose whether or not it's shallow would depend on the situation and one's heart."

"It always goes back to the motives of the heart." Tara remembered the words that had stuck with her all week. "Where your treasure is, there will your heart be also."

"Jesus did say that, and there is a lot of truth to it." Mrs. Carpenter poured herself a cup of hot coffee from the stove, then sat at the table. "I've worked on this farm for almost forty years, and while I can't begin to do what I did when I was younger, for a long time I believed what I did was completely unimportant. What good is milking a cow every morning or the endless gathering of eggs from the chickens?"

Tara grinned. "Believe it or not, I've started to find satisfaction in such chores, but I see your point. That's exactly how I've been feeling. As though nothing I do is enough."

The older woman took a sip of her coffee

before adding a spoonful of sugar. "I spent years longing to accomplish something heroic for God, and I was never happy with who I was. Then I learned something from a dear friend of mine that has stuck with me for years. I might long to accomplish something big that the world sees as impressive, but what's even more important is that I approach every day's household tasks and duties as if they were indeed just as valuable. To spend each day as if I were doing everything for Christ Himself."

Tara leaned back against the counter. "That's quite a profound statement."

"Jesus said as much when He told us to seek first His kingdom and His righteousness, and all these things shall be added unto us. It's always been a matter of the heart."

Tara knew Mrs. Carpenter was right. She'd been so obsessed with her mission that she'd neglected her own relationship with God. And, as hard as it was to admit it, she knew she needed to work on getting her heart right with God and get her treasure in the right place. But surely, that didn't make what she was doing wrong.

Or did it?

"God looks at our heart," the older woman continued. "The motives behind our actions, whether it's a big task like Moses leading the Israelites across the Red Sea or a simple one like cleaning out a horse stall for God's glory. If you've ever read through the Old Testament, it's amazing at how God looks on the inside before He ever looks at what we have accomplished."

Tara pressed her fingertips together. "It reminds me of Sampson. Always whistling a cheerful tune even when he's mucking a stall."

She knew there was nothing innately wrong with her quest for gold. But her motives had become self-seeking. That's where the problem lay. Now all she had to do was figure out how to set things right with God.

Aaron watched as Miss Young entered the hotel restaurant; then he breathed out a sigh of relief. He stood as she approached his table, trying to ignore how lovely she looked. Her blue dress, with its contrasting white trim, highlighted her eyes, and her hair, pinned up neatly beneath one of her fancy hats, was now back to its normal shade of auburn.

He pulled out her chair and waited for her to be seated. "I wasn't sure you'd come."

She gave him a shy grin. "You made it a bit hard for me to refuse. New information

170

and a proposition? Sounds like a bit of a truce."

"You could say that."

Aaron sat down and laid his Stetson on the table. He shouldn't feel so pleased that she was sitting across from him at one of the restaurant's corner tables, or that he was about to ask her for assistance in a government matter. But he couldn't help it. He'd wanted to see her again. Wanted to continue their conversations on farming, art, and spiritual matters. To simply spend the afternoon getting to know her better without the gold coming between them.

However, that wasn't why he was here. Nothing had really changed. He planned to ask for her help — beg, if need be, to get his job done. And once he found the gold, or some sort of proof that it couldn't be recovered, then he'd take on the next assignment. Or retire to some rolling hillside near the banks of the Mississippi. Alone.

"I . . . thanks for coming." He pressed his lips together, determined not to get tongue-tied today. "What would you like to drink?"

Miss Young set her light wrap on the chair behind her. "Lemonade would be wonderful."

Aaron motioned for the waitress and ordered them each a glass before continuing their conversation. "It's hot today, isn't it?"

"Very." She smiled and his heart tripped. "But I still enjoyed the drive here. The fields are sprinkled with Queen Anne's lace and the perfume of wild roses."

"And there are clouds in the horizon." He tugged on his collar, longing for relief from the stifling heat. A light breeze filtered in from the open front door but did little to alleviate the humid air. "I believe we're in for some wet weather. Might help cool things down."

"Mr. Carpenter said the crops could use another good rain. He's afraid production will be down this year."

The waitress put tall glasses of lemonade in front of them, then headed back to the kitchen. At two o'clock in the afternoon the place was quiet with no other patrons, which was exactly what he'd counted on. What they had to discuss had to be kept between them.

"For a city girl, you've learned a lot since your arrival in Iowa." He caught her gaze, grateful for the few minutes of small talk before things between them got serious. "You need to be careful, though."

"And why is that?"

"For instance, wild parsnip is often mistaken for Queen Anne's lace, but the wild parsnip is a rather toxic plant that can actually burn the skin if one isn't careful. Things aren't always what they appear to be."

"Apparently, I have much to learn." She cocked her head. "Does that apply to people, as well?"

"In my line of work, I've found that one must always be cautious."

Aaron toyed with the cloth napkin. Looking at her heart-shaped face and full lips, it was easy to forget the real reason he was here. He shifted his gaze to the decorative wallpaper behind her. Swirls of lavender blurred before him as he tried to refocus on the matter at hand. He wasn't here because the woman sitting across from him made him want to retire and settle down. He was here to make a deal and find the gold.

"Is there anything else I should watch out for?"

He blinked at her question and turned back to her. Was there anything else to watch out for? Here was a woman who'd been attacked, shot at, threatened, and had somehow even managed to color her hair purple. If anything, people needed to watch out when they were around *her*.

He shook his head. But she'd been talking about plants. Queen Anne's lace . . .

roses . . . "To watch out for what?"

"You mentioned wild parsnip."

"Oh. I don't know . . ." He shook his head and tried to think. "Poison ivy, stinging nettle, and the black locust tree, I suppose, for starters."

She smiled at him. "I didn't know you were interested in such matters."

"My grandfather taught me a love and a respect for the land."

"But we're not here to discuss plants, are we?" She looked around the empty room then leaned forward. "I'm anxious to know what information you have to share with me."

Aaron cleared his throat. She was right. It was time to get to the issue at hand. "I found out yesterday that Mr. Schlosser is dead."

Miss Young drew in a sharp breath, and he cringed. He hadn't meant to be so blunt. He'd found himself so wrapped up in her presence that he knew he needed to forge past all the small talk or he'd find the afternoon spent with no progress made. But what happened to his skills of diplomacy and discretion? If he had any hope of getting what he wanted, then he would have to be careful how he said things.

"I'm sorry." He picked up his lemonade

and let the small chunks of ice swirl in the glass. "It came as quite a shock to me, as well. I was hoping that your lead would pay off."

"I'm just surprised." She took a sip of her drink. "This changes things substantially."

"It means that we are both out of leads. Unless . . ." He let his voice trail off. He had to sound convincing. "Unless we work together."

Her eyes widened. "You want me to help you?"

"You have information. I have the resources. Together, we might actually be able to recover the gold."

He liked the thought of them working together. He couldn't help it. A lonely retirement wasn't an appealing future. As hard as he'd tried not to, she was the one he saw sitting beside him on a porch swing watching the sunrise or on a cold winter evening in front of the fireplace.

"What about the reward money?" She eyed him cautiously. "Would you still be willing to make good on it?"

"Of course."

She lowered her gaze. "I know what you're thinking, and I don't want you to believe that I'm completely self-centered."

He wasn't sure what she meant. "I don't."

She frowned "It's really not about the money."

"Then what is it about?"

She stared at her glass and began wiping away the condensation. "It's about proving I can do something worthwhile in life."

"I don't understand."

Miss Young folded her hands on the table and looked at him. "My aunt was a spy for the Union in the war. She made a difference, risking her life while passing important information to key people. My parents were a part of the Underground Railroad. They helped countless people escaping from slavery. And as for myself . . ." She shrugged. "I've failed to do anything of value."

Aaron shook his head, wondering how a beautiful and intelligent woman could think such a thing about herself. "But you told me about your charity work and —"

"What good is giving a child a blanket or a pair of shoes, when you can't assure him that he will one day have a home where he is loved?" An underlying passion resonated through her voice as she gripped the edge of the table. "What assurance is it to give a cup of soup to someone one day when the next day she'll still be hungry? Everything I've done is small. Insignificant. I want to do something . . . something big with my life."

Aaron was surprised at her display of honesty, but he also understood exactly where she was coming from. Hadn't he spent his whole life searching for the same things? Yearning to find a way to measure up to someone else's standard. There was one thing, though, that wasn't clear in his mind.

He longed to understand completely what was in her heart. "You say you want to make a difference to people, but how does finding the gold accomplish that?"

"I don't know." She fidgeted in her chair. "I read my aunt's journals after hearing her stories while she was still living. Finding the gold seemed like something tangible I could do to help my country. A silly idea, wasn't it —"

"No." He reached out and squeezed her hand, then pulled back at the intimate gesture. He had no right to bridge that gap between them. And he mustn't forget that their relationship was strictly business. "I'm sorry, but no. I don't think your actions were foolish. Not at all."

Miss Young's gaze rested on the hand that he had touched. "They were foolish, and you know it."

He folded his arms across his chest. "I think you're wrong."

"How can you understand how I feel?" She shook her head, and he didn't miss the tears that pooled in the corners of her eyes. "You've spent your life making this country a better place by bringing criminals to justice and stopping evil men from following through with their plans. You've made a difference."

Aaron winced. Her words might seem true to someone looking at his life from the outside, but to him, his actions had never been enough. At least not enough in the eyes of some.

"Have you ever thought about what God sees as success and failure?"

He stopped to consider her question, though it wasn't something he hadn't thought of before. He'd wondered the very same thing a dozen times. Did his hard work make up for his failures in God's eyes? It was a question to which he'd never found the answer.

"I'm not sure, but I doubt He sees things the way we do."

"Do you have an example?"

He wasn't following her train of thought. "An example?"

"From the Bible. I just thought of the

widow who gave her last two coins to the offering. Man saw that as foolish, but Jesus held her up as an example because He saw how her motives were pure compared to the rich and their large offerings." She leaned forward, intent. "Jesus saw the motivations of the woman's heart, not how much she gave."

"You're right."

He'd spent his whole life worrying about the external results and far too little time examining his heart and what really mattered. The significance of what she said was sobering. An image of Jesus on the cross flashed before him. Christ was the one Man who'd never concerned Himself with what the world said or thought about Him. Instead, He'd spent His time on earth teaching the truth. And none of it had been what the people expected.

"What about the life of Jesus?" he offered. "To the world, don't you think His life was a failure? Not only did all His followers leave Him, the mob had Him crucified. But God saw success in Christ's sufferings on the cross even when everyone else heralded the event as a complete failure."

She nodded. "God knew the final outcome. And the fact that Jesus would conquer death. And that's why He looks at our hearts. It doesn't matter if we're parting the Red Sea or cleaning out a horse stall."

"What?"

She laughed for the first time all afternoon. "Or shall I say that whether we're chasing a pot of gold or a band of outlaws for a living, it isn't as important as whether or not we are following Him with our whole heart."

He matched her broad grin. "I'd say you're exactly right."

"I have the journal. I suppose you'd like to look at it."

"You wouldn't mind?"

She shook her head. "And besides, our conversation has given me an idea."

# THIRTEEN

Tara read through the last few verses of Romans chapter eight, then laid her Bible on the small table beside the rocking chair. She took a deep breath. From the front porch of the Carpenters' home, the air was fragrant with the sweet-smelling honeysuckle that grew along the side of the house. It had rained all night, bringing a renewed freshness to the morning temperature. For the first time in months, she felt surrounded by a warm blanket of contentment.

She ran her fingers across the leather-bound Bible her parents had given her on her sixteenth birthday. Verse thirty-seven in particular had stood out during her devotional. Paul had written that in all things we are more than conquerors through Him that loved us. The straightforward words were significant, especially in the light of her conversation with Mr. Jefferson yesterday.

Aaron Jefferson.

Just the thought of his name made her smile. The man continued to amaze her. Rarely had she met someone willing to discuss spiritual matters in such a forthright and honest way. And while he seemed to be grappling with his own uncertainties, his sincerity in discovering God's will for his life was evident. And his example of Christ's death as the ultimate victory out of perceived failure was key.

It was a situation that didn't make sense to the world. Life through death. Success through sacrifice. Storing up treasures in heaven and not on this world. But God's Word was clear. Only through Christ would she be able to find her worth. The reminder was freeing. And one she regretted not grasping sooner. When she'd made the decision to give her life to Christ, she had confessed He was Lord and had been baptized into His death in order to live a new life. It was time she started fully living that position as the daughter of the King. Time she stopped worrying about how the world saw her.

She knew now that she didn't have to find the gold to be worth something in God's eyes. Christ wanted her to daily live for Him, no matter what she was doing. He'd accepted the widow's small gift as if it were all of Solomon's wealth. And He would accept all her offerings, gifts, and talents as she used them for His glory. He just wanted her undivided heart.

A horse and rider galloping down the dusty lane toward the Carpenters' home caught her attention. Tara stood and put her hand above her eyes to shield the morning sun. The older couple hadn't mentioned that they were expecting company, though an occasional visit from the pastor or one of the other members of the church wasn't uncommon.

Or maybe Mr. Jefferson had decided to call on her this morning instead of waiting to meet again at the hotel restaurant with her aunt's journal as he'd suggested. The thought of seeing him now made her heart flutter, and she strained for a view of his ever-present Stetson.

The rider slowed as he approached the house, but this man wasn't wearing a black hat. She wrapped her hand around the porch's solid post. Faded denim jeans paired with a worn plaid shirt . . .

It wasn't Mr. Jefferson. It was Mr. Martin.

The man stopped in front of the house and slid off his chestnut mount. He tipped his hat, but his expression was far from friendly. "Good day, Miss Young."

"Mr. Martin." Tara clasped her hands together. "I wasn't expecting to see you today."

"I'm sure you weren't." The man's gaze scanned the front of the house while his hand rested on his sidearm. Either he had news regarding their quest for papers Mr. Schlosser had left behind, or the man was here on other business. From his somber expression, something made her fear the latter.

She attempted to keep a smile in her voice. "Is there something I can do for you today?"

He stopped at the bottom of the staircase. "Where are the Carpenters?"

"Inside, finishing their morning coffee." Tara felt her lip twitch. "Why —"

"Is anyone else around?"

Sampson had gone into town for supplies. Even the nearest tenant farmer was likely to be out of earshot.

"I can't say for sure."

He pulled a gun out of his holster and marched up the stairs. "I want you to take me to the Carpenters. Now."

Tara couldn't move. She stared at the gun and tried to breathe slowly so she wouldn't faint. What had the scripture said this morning?

*Who shall separate us from the love of Christ? Shall tribulation, or distress —*

"I believe I gave you an order, Miss Young."

Tara moved to open the front door, praying each step of the way. The verse continued to flow through her mind. *Or persecution, or famine, or nakedness, or peril, or sword — or gun . . . Nay, in all these things we are more than conquerors through him that loved us.*

*Through Christ.*

"Where are they?" Mr. Martin's voice reverberated through the quiet house.

Repeating the verse in her mind, she led him through the kitchen and into the dining area with the large window overlooking the back pasture.

"Tara?" Mr. Carpenter's smile vanished as he moved to stand, but Mr. Martin shoved him back in the chair.

Tara sat across from the Carpenters as ordered. "I'm sorry. He has a gun."

The cozy dining room, where they had shared dozens of meals over the past few weeks, seemed suddenly cold. Even the warming summer sun couldn't take away the chill she felt. Mrs. Carpenter grabbed onto her husband's arm, her eyes widening in fear.

He set his coffee mug on the table and clasped his wife's hand. "What do you want?"

"Where's Mr. Jefferson?"

Tara tried to speak, but fear seeped through every pore of her body. Mr. Jefferson had been right. She seemed to have a knack for attracting trouble. Except this time, she had no idea what she'd just gotten herself into.

"I asked you a question, Miss Young." Mr. Martin smacked his hand against the table.

Tara jumped. "He's . . . I don't know. In town somewhere, I suppose. I haven't seen him today."

She squeezed her eyes shut for a moment. *We are more than conquerors. We are more than conquerors.* She repeated the words over and over and tried to get a grip on the panic enveloping her.

Mr. Martin pointed the gun out the window as he paced the room and scanned the horizon.

*Neither death, nor life . . . nor height, nor death . . . shall be able to separate us from the love of God.*

Scenes flashed through Tara's mind of times she'd longed to do something bold

186

and heroic. This time, she knew she didn't have to prove anything. Inside her being, as a child of God, was a far greater source of strength than anything she could ever have on her own. Silently, she began to pray, until the fear faded into a dim image of what it had been before.

"Mr. Martin?"

He turned to face her. "What?"

She sat up straight and looked him in the eye. "I'm sorry our visit the other day upset you. I'm assuming that's what this about?"

He took a step toward her and shook his head. "How can you act as if you have no idea? You came into my house with the pretense of finding a stack of letters that belonged to your aunt, when what you really wanted to do was to set a trap for me. I'm not stupid."

"Of course you're not." Tara worked to keep her voice calm. "This is about your wife, isn't it?"

"Matilda." For an instant his face softened. "Matilda Grace Martin. I loved her so much."

"I'm sure you did." Tara measured each word she spoke. "I saw her picture. She was beautiful."

The man let out a forced laugh. "She never thought so. She was thin and never had the energy to do very much. No one understood except for me. I told her that I didn't care if she couldn't work the farm like the other women. I would just work twice as hard."

Tara nodded slowly. "She was sick?"

He turned to her, obviously surprised by her comment. But Tara knew her words were not her own. And the peace she was experiencing at the moment could come only from God and not her own wisdom.

"I never should have brought her here." He rubbed his chin and walked back to the window. "I thought a change might help. A place of our own where she could breathe fresh air like the doctors back east told us. Nothing I did helped her. She just kept getting weaker and weaker until one day she couldn't even get out of bed."

Tara watched the slight changes in Mr. Martin as the sadness of losing his wife began to replace his focused anger. "I'm so sorry."

Mrs. Carpenter leaned forward. "But you said she went back east to stay with her mother."

Mr. Martin's jaw tensed. "You were just like the others. You never cared —"

"That's not true."

Tara held up her hand. "Where is your

wife, Mr. Martin?"

He shook his head and began pacing along the window. "I won't go to jail. My land is the only thing I have left of her, and I can't leave."

"No one is asking you to leave, Mr. Martin."

"Don't lie to me." He waved the gun in the air, and the hard lines returned to his face. "That's why you came. I know it. You and Mr. Jefferson. Snooping around, asking questions. You came to take me to jail."

"No, we came looking for Mr. Schlosser. That's the truth. I'm terribly sorry about your wife. I know it must hurt so much to be away from her."

Mr. Martin's hand began to shake. "I killed her."

Tara felt a wave of shock rush through here. "You killed your wife?"

"I didn't mean to, but I killed her."

"She was sick, Mr. Martin, and she died. Isn't that right?"

"She was so sick. But I couldn't save her. I tried. I wanted to make her better, but one day she didn't wake up." He pressed the side of the gun against his forehead and groaned. "I buried her on my land so I could be close to her. But I couldn't tell anyone. They would think that I was a bad man. That I belonged in jail like my father."

"No one thinks you killed your wife. It's going to be all right." Tara stood up slowly. "Give me the gun, Mr. Martin. We don't want anyone to accidentally get hurt. I know you don't want that. You're not that kind of man."

His lowered his hand, but he didn't let go of the gun. His gaze shifted toward the front door. "No. I can't. It's a trap."

His expression hardened as he turned to her, held up the gun, and pointed it at her heart.

# FOURTEEN

Aaron paced the hotel lobby, waiting for Miss Young's arrival. She was an hour late, and if his fears were correct, she'd just stood him up. Rotating the brim of his Stetson between his fingers, he stopped in front of the narrow plate of glass that overlooked the street. The boardwalk was busy with morning shoppers, but there was no sign of the impulsive young woman with auburn hair who'd stepped into his life and managed to turn it upside down.

One thing in particular had him worried. What if she had found something in her aunt's journal after their discussion and decided to proceed with the search on her own? The very idea made his stomach turn. Knowing Miss Young, she'd end up in yet another fix. And this time, he might not be there to save her.

He pulled his watch from his trouser pocket and opened the case to check the time once more. She was now an hour and five minutes late.

"Constantly checking the time rarely makes it pass any faster, Mr. Jefferson."

Aaron spun around on the heels of his boots. Mrs. Meddler, the hotel owner's wife, stood there, observing him with her typical inquisitive gaze. Far from attractive, with her narrow face and too-thin nose, the woman's one pleasant feature was her jovial personality, but even that quality, he'd discovered at their first meeting, was overbearing at times.

"Is she late?" Mrs. Meddler folded her hands across her well-endowed form and smiled.

He scratched the back of his head. "Who?"

"Miss Young, of course."

It would seem that nothing got past the woman. Aaron cleared his throat. "I . . . well . . . yes, but we were only meeting for business."

Mrs. Meddler nodded, the grin never leaving her face. "I'm sure from what I witnessed yesterday in the restaurant that you are correct. Strictly business. Of course, that doesn't explain the slight blush that stained her face every time you looked at her, or the way you stuttered whenever she asked you a question."

Aaron's eyes widened at the unsolicited observation. The woman seemed to be everywhere. Perhaps she should be the one working for the government. He was obviously losing his touch.

He closed his eyes for a moment and struggled to gain back his composure. "Mrs. Meddler —"

"It's all right to admit it." Her eyes held a hint of amusement.

"Admit what?" If it was possible, the woman exasperated him more than Miss Young did. He'd never been one to avoid the issue at hand. He wanted the facts presented up front, but she had him running in circles like a decapitated rooster in a barnyard.

"Admit that you're attracted to her." Mrs. Meddler waved her finger at him. "That perhaps you even have feelings for her. Miss Young is a lovely young woman, with a heart for God and others. You couldn't do any better."

He slapped his hat against his trouser leg and pressed his lips together before speaking. "You've forgotten one small detail, Mrs. Meddler. I don't even know her. Every time I've seen her has been surrounded by mayhem and disaster. Not exactly the environment for courtship . . . if that was what I was looking for, which I'm not."

"Oh? I didn't hear any gunshots or see any signs of trouble in the restaurant yesterday while the two of you were here." Mrs. Meddler let out a soft sigh and shook her head. "No, on the contrary, the atmosphere was quite ideal. But perhaps my husband is correct when he tells me that I read far too many dime novels and have my head in the clouds, but I can tell love when I see it —"

"Love?" Aaron coughed. Now her comments had crossed the line from inquisitive to intrusive.

He bit down on his tongue so he wouldn't say something foolish. He didn't have feelings for the young woman, let alone feelings of love. Why, the very idea was preposterous. The woman got herself into trouble every time she turned around. She needed a bodyguard, not a husband, because she was impulsive, rash, and reckless.

No. He had no intentions of falling for Miss Young, or even discussing her for that matter.

Mrs. Meddler stepped forward. Apparently she wasn't finished. "I did have to laugh the day I saw her wearing your black Stetson on her head as she strode down the boardwalk. It was yours, wasn't it?"

"My Stetson?" He glanced at his hat and

frowned.

What was the woman referring to now? His mind went back to the day they'd been shot at outside the post office. He'd lost his hat, and Miss Young had been the one to return it, but he couldn't imagine her wearing it. Mrs. Meddler was obviously incorrect. Too many of those made-up tales not only had her head in the clouds, they'd also clouded her eyesight.

He shook his head. He would never figure out the reason Miss Young would have been wearing his Stetson, so there was no use trying. "Mrs. Meddler, I must protest. I am simply meeting Miss Young to discuss business relating to my work for the government. She has some information for me . . ."

Aaron sucked in a deep breath. Splendid. Not only was he coming close to losing his temper, he was giving away too much information, as well.

*Because the woman's right.*

She's right? He shoved the thought aside. The woman was certainly not correct in her assessment. He was going to go straight to the Carpenter farm to find Miss Young so he could finish his business and leave town. And the sooner he left the better.

He took a step toward the door. "Mrs.

Meddler, if you will excuse me, I need to go now."

She smiled again as he turned to leave. "Please give my regards to Miss Young and have her stop by for tea at her earliest convenience. I do so enjoy her company."

Aaron gave her a curt nod, then strode down the boardwalk toward the livery. He normally wasn't one to get frustrated so easily, but that woman was intent on putting ideas in his head. Ideas that he had no time for analyzing.

*Because it's the truth and you know it.*

He grunted and shoved his hat onto his head. There was no way around it. He had to concede defeat. As much as he longed to admit that Mrs. Meddler was only an interfering busybody with her pointed words and attempts at matchmaking, his heart knew that she was at least partially correct. Love might be too strong a word, but what was the use denying the truth? Miss Tara Young had waltzed into his life like an unexpected afternoon rain shower and left everything a bit brighter. He couldn't deny it. Despite the trouble that seemed to follow wherever she went, she'd managed to work her way right into the middle of his heart.

Swiftly saddling his stallion at the livery, he made his way toward the Carpenter farmhouse, his thoughts in a muddled jumble. Why was it, when dealing with a woman — when dealing with Miss Young — logic and rational thinking seemed to vanish? He had no idea what he was going to say to her, or even if he should say something to her. He had no time for courting even if his heart was intent on winning this round.

As he approached the Carpenters' house, he could already see the subtle changes that had transformed the double-story dwelling. The flower beds in the front had been trimmed and weeded, and the front porch now sported a brand-new coat of white paint. He was quite certain that the improvements had all been made under the watchful eye of Miss Young.

A horse was tethered beside the porch, and if he wasn't mistaken, it didn't belong to the Carpenters. An uneasy feeling tried to surface, but he pushed aside the worrisome thought. Just because Miss Young had a knack for trouble didn't mean there was anything wrong this morning. The Carpenters simply had a visitor.

Dismounting from his stallion, he started up the front porch steps, then stopped. After years of being a lawman he couldn't ignore the warning signs. Surely his overcautious feelings were nothing more than an acknowledgement of the fact that Miss Young was involved. That alone should make him more cautious. But the fact remained. Something wasn't right. A visitor would mean tea and coffee in the front parlor, or perhaps on the front porch, and what he saw through the sitting room windows confirmed that the area was empty.

Aaron made his way along the front porch. Even if he was wrong, erring on the side of caution had rarely left him off target. He moved silently toward the side of the house. The scent of honeysuckle filled his senses, and he struggled not to sneeze. He held his breath until the unsettled feeling passed, then stepped up alongside the dining room.

A man stood with his back to the window . . . and he held a gun. A stab of fear pierced through Aaron's gut. The balding man turned his head slightly, giving Aaron a clear view of the man's profile.

James Martin.

Making sure he stayed as close to the house as possible, Aaron pushed aside the panic and took another side step to confirm who else was in the room. Miss Young stood across from the gunman. He caught her gaze through the window. He saw the subtle shake of her head and frowned. He wasn't sure what she meant, but there was no way he wasn't getting involved in the situation. It was too late for that. Especially when the person Mr. Martin was holding the gun on the woman he loved.

Loved?

Aaron grunted. Mrs. Meddler had apparently been right on all accounts. He, with all his strong notions of finishing his job without any further distractions, had fallen in love with Miss Young. But before he let plans of courting fill his mind, he needed a plan. He was going to have to be careful, for one false move and he was certain Mr. Martin was unstable enough that he would pull the trigger. And Miss Young certainly wasn't skilled enough in the art of negotiation so that she could remedy the situation on her own.

But if anything happened to her . . .

Aaron moved swiftly toward the back of the house and, feeling completely out of control for the first time in his life, he began to pray.

Tara's heart pounded at the sight of Mr. Jefferson. Thankfully, Mr. Martin hadn't seemed to have noticed her attempts to convey a message. All she needed was Mr. Jefferson to burst his way into the room and spook Mr. Martin. She was quite certain that with one false move, Mr. Martin would fire his pistol. And it was aimed straight at her.

Mr. Martin had spent the past hour talking about his wife, her sickness, and how no one had seemed to care about their situation. Knowing many of the good people of Browning City, Tara was quite certain that wasn't true, but it was clearly his interpretation of the situation. The Carpenters had said little during the ordeal, which was best. There was no use aggravating the man further.

Tara glanced again at the window, but Mr. Jefferson had disappeared. Undoubtedly, he'd assumed that she had stood him up and had come after her to make sure she didn't further pursue the gold without him. He had nothing to worry about. With a gun pointed at her for the past hour, she wasn't going anywhere.

She was also quite certain that he was, right now, coming up with a plan to rescue her and the Carpenters. With a gun in Mr. Martin's hand, though, there was little chance that such an action could succeed without someone getting hurt. It was time to put an end to this.

Sending up another prayer, she stood

slowly, her gaze never leaving her captor's. "I can't change the past, Mr. Martin, but I can help you change the future."

Aaron opened the back door and tried to remember the layout of the rectangular farmhouse. His options were limited. The sitting room and the Carpenters' bedroom were in the front of the house, while the kitchen and dining area made up the back half. A partial wall separated the dining area from the kitchen, giving him cover until he had to make his presence known. But from experience he knew the setup wouldn't allow a surprise attack.

Setting his Stetson on the counter, he crouched on the wooden floor planks and prayed for an answer. He needed a distraction, but what? With Mr. Martin holding the gun less than six feet from Miss Young, he couldn't take a chance of startling the man. Even if he had bad aim, the chances were still too great that he would hit her.

He needed control of the situation. But that was the one thing he didn't have. And he didn't foresee any changes right away. He heard voices in the next room. Miss Young's soft, soothing voice and Mr. Martin's raspy responses.

He was out of options.

*What do I do, God?*

Aaron waited for a response, an idea, anything that would get her and the Carpenters out . . . alive. His brow began to sweat. His stomach churned. He was used to pushing his way in and taking charge of a situation, not waiting around for the situation to diffuse on its own. Or in this case, explode from the barrel of a gun.

That was the option he couldn't handle. He couldn't stand by and do nothing, yet rushing in would only bring disaster.

Aaron cried out again to God. *I need your help, Lord. I need You. What do I do?*

The question struck him. He balanced on the heels of his boots and studied a knot in the grain on the floor. Its texture was rough and jagged. Like the edges of his heart. When was the last time he'd stopped and asked God for guidance? When was the last time he hadn't simply forged ahead on his own and instead sat quietly listening for his Savior's answer? He'd been so wrapped up in proving himself and trying to live up to his name that he'd failed to let his relationship with Christ guide him.

Miss Young's question at the restaurant struck him again. *Have you ever thought about what God sees as success and failure?*

He'd wanted success, and had worked

hard at it until the desire permeated every aspect of his life. He knew there was nothing wrong with his chosen profession, except that he'd put it above his relationship with Christ. The fact that Jesus Himself had given up success in order to bring the world salvation convicted him. Christ had worked to please only one person in life. His heavenly Father. Even to the point of taking on the sins of the world and allowing Himself to be sacrificed for the sake of a lost world.

Everything led back to the cross, and what his Savior had done for him.

*Oh Lord, I've wandered so far from Your presence in search of my own success and earthly treasures. Help me to find You again.*

"Mr. Jefferson? You can come in here now."

Aaron froze. Miss Young's voice sounded shaky as she called from the other room. He hesitated. What if it was a trap, and Mr. Martin was forcing her to call him into the room?

"Really, everything's all right now." She stepped into the kitchen with the gun in her hand pointing toward the floor.

He walked toward her. "How'd you know I was here? And the gun . . ."

Her voice was shaky and her face pale,

but the relief in her eyes was clear. "I knew you'd come to my rescue, but there weren't many options in this situation. I also knew that I was the one who was going to have to talk Mr. Martin into giving me the gun. Somehow, God gave me the words to say."

She dropped the weapon into his hand and leaned against the counter. He wrapped his arms around her waist, afraid she might collapse. Something told him, though, that she was stronger than he'd ever imagined.

The Carpenters entered the kitchen behind her. Mr. Carpenter's hand rested possessively around his wife's shoulder.

Aaron held Miss Young steady as he addressed the older couple. "Are you both all right?"

"Yes." Mr. Carpenter shook Aaron's free hand. "But we'd be obliged if you would take Mr. Martin in to the sheriff. If it hadn't been for Tara and her well-spoken words, well, I don't know what would have happened."

Miss Young shook her head. "Today, they were God's words. Never mine."

"Then God was speaking mighty powerfully. You saved our lives." He nodded his head in thanks. "I'm going to take the missus here to go sit down. It was quite a scare for us both."

As the Carpenters left the room, Aaron glanced at Mr. Martin. He sat in a chair in the corner of the room, a glazed expression on his face. The man wasn't going anywhere for the moment.

Aaron turned back to Miss Young. A rosy blush had returned to her cheeks, and he wasn't certain if it was from the relief that the situation was over or from his nearness. He hoped it was because she shared the same feelings toward him he felt toward her.

"Mr. Jefferson —"

He pushed back an errant curl that hung across her cheek. "I think after all we've been through together, it's time you called me by my first name. Do you mind?"

"Not at all . . . Aaron."

He liked the sound of her voice when she said his name. And liked the feel of her in his arms.

"And please, call me Tara."

He nodded. There was so much he wanted to tell her, but he was going to first have to get Mr. Martin to the sheriff's office and give her a chance to catch her breath after the ordeal.

"There's one other thing you might want to know." Tara looked up at him, her eyes wide with anticipation. "While we were talking, Mr. Martin showed me letters he'd found belonging to Mr. Schlosser. They were from my aunt."

# FIFTEEN

Tara felt her knees tremble, but this time it wasn't from fear. She grabbed onto the counter to steady herself. Mr. Jefferson — Aaron's — gaze hadn't left her face, and there was something in his eyes she couldn't ignore. From their first few encounters, she'd noted his interest in her despite their opposing goals, but there was something different lurking in the depths of his eyes today. Something deeper and more intense.

Could it be true that his feelings went further than mere attraction?

He fumbled with his hat between his hands. "I need to take Mr. Martin into town. Are you going to be all right?"

She nodded, not sure if she could speak anymore. "I . . . yes. I'll be fine."

He raised his hand toward her face as if he was going to stroke her cheek, then pulled his arm down. "I'd best be going."

"Are you coming back?" She followed him

into the dining area, conscious of the desperation in her voice, but unable to control it.

"Give me time to get him to the sheriff's office, and I'll return." He rested his Stetson on his head. "We can look over the letters together."

From the Carpenters' front porch, she watched as he escorted Mr. Martin along the edge of the cornfield until they disappeared into the hazy horizon. She swallowed her disappointment. Part of her had longed for Aaron to stay and pull her back into his arms where she'd felt safe. To tell her how relieved he was she hadn't been hurt.

Instead he'd promised to return . . . to see the letters.

Tara leaned against the wooden banister and tugged on the edge of her jacket. The endless fields of corn and apple orchards that had grown tiresome during the journey to Iowa and the first weeks that followed seemed to have taken on a richer hue. She took in a deep breath of the fresh air that brought with it the fragrance of honeysuckle and the rich scent of the fertile earth that made this land a farmer's dream. A recent letter from her parents had urged her to return home to the ease of city life, but thoughts of what she had in Boston were coming fewer and further between. Just as Aaron had somehow stolen a corner of her heart, the vast state of Iowa had managed to do the same thing.

She could imagine staying . . . with him.

Tara shook her head and crossed the wide porch toward the front door. Truth was, it didn't matter what the handsome lawman felt toward her. She might have noted a change in his expression, but something else, far more important, had just changed in her own life.

For the first time, she'd managed to completely trust in God and had faced her fears. The result had been greater than finding a stash of gold. What she'd experienced might not have had as far-reaching consequences as her aunt spying for the North or her parents' involvement with the Underground Railroad, but nevertheless, her own actions had made a difference in the lives of three other people. Most importantly, she was struck with God's faithfulness in the situation. Her words to Mr. Martin had not come from her own wisdom and understanding. God had given her the grace and courage she had needed for the moment.

"Tara?"

She stepped inside the house where the

Carpenters sat side by side on the sofa. Mr. Carpenter's arm was wrapped protectively around his wife, whose face was still paler than a winter's snowfall.

Tara paused in the entryway, her hands clasped tightly in front of her. She was worried. While she knew the couple to be resilient, such an ordeal, especially at their age, couldn't be good for their well-being. "Are you both all right?"

Mr. Carpenter held his gold watch between the fingers of his free hand and continued to click the cover open and shut. "Only time I've been this scared is when Sam Barnett burst into our Sunday night prayer meeting with a rifle in his hands and whiskey on his breath. Poor Virginia. I thought the woman was going to faint over her husband's scandalous behavior. Turned out, all he wanted was supper on the table. A few too many drinks had wrecked his thinkin'."

Mrs. Carpenter frowned and nudged her husband with her elbow. "Gossip aside, we need to thank the good Lord it's over."

"You're right." Tara sat across from them on a worn chair. And at least no one had been shot . . . or fainted during today's arduous situation. Including herself. "Mr. Jefferson is taking Mr. Martin to the sheriff's office. I thought I'd make you both a cup of tea if you'd like. It might help you to relax."

"That would be wonderful, dear." Mrs. Carpenter leaned into her husband's shoulder. "Looks to me as if today turned out to be a bit more exciting than collecting the eggs, wouldn't you think?"

Tara placed her hand against her chest and let out a low chuckle, thankful for the lighter turn of the conversation. "I've decided that if I end up spending the rest of my life collecting eggs and milking cows, that will be thrill enough for me."

Color began to come back into the older woman's face. "Sometimes being heroic in God's eyes simply means listening quietly and following His voice. Which is precisely what I saw you do with Mr. Martin."

Tara shrugged a shoulder. "I don't feel heroic by any means, but I can't help but be reminded of the passage I read last night when God appeared to Elijah. The prophet waited through the violent wind, earthquakes, and even a fire to find God, yet He wasn't in any of those."

Mr. Carpenter nodded. "Instead He was in the gentle whisper many of us miss."

"I've always believed that I had to do something big to serve God." Pieces of the puzzle Tara had been struggling with for weeks began to come together. "I don't know if I feel heroic, but I did hear God's quiet whisper today."

Mrs. Carpenter reached out to squeeze Tara's hand. "Then you've learned a wise lesson that many fail to ever realize."

Tara stood to start toward the kitchen, her thoughts still focused on their discussion. "I'll go and make some tea now."

"Tara?"

She turned back to face Mrs. Carpenter. "Yes?"

"Thank you for what you did today."

Aaron approached the Carpenters' farm, hopeful that his entire life was about to change. No longer did he care what the letters contained. True, he would soon find out whether Miss Young — Tara's — information regarding the gold would pan out or not, but his mind was focused on other things. He smiled at the thought of her name. Tara. The name was beautiful, but not nearly as beautiful as the woman who wore it. For the first time in months, he'd found something worthwhile to pursue. Something far greater than the gold that he had chased after for so long.

Tara sat on the front porch, engrossed in something.

The letters.

His heart plummeted for an instant. What if her involvement with him reached no further than the gold? He'd know soon enough. Her face lit up when she saw him, bringing with it a sigh of relief on his part. No, he couldn't be wrong. He'd seen the way she looked at him. It wasn't simply about the gold.

Aaron dismounted from his horse, tethered the reins, then took the porch stairs two at a time. "Hi."

"Hi." She looked up at him and smiled.

He balanced his Stetson on one of the porch posts. Color once again tinged her cheeks. The fear that had edged her eyes had disappeared, leaving them bright and hopeful. She looked beautiful.

He shoved his hands into his pockets and rocked back on his heels. "You'll be glad to know that Mr. Martin is behind bars and will no doubt go to trial at some point."

"I feel sorry for the man." His assurances hadn't brought about the continued smile he expected from her. "I think he's overcome by the loss of his wife. He must have loved her so much. It's heartbreaking, really."

"True." Aaron sat down beside her on one of the rocking chairs. "But the fact remains that we can't take a chance that he does something like that again and shoots someone."

"I suppose you're right." She held up the stack of letters. "I read through them."

"And . . ."

No matter how hard his pulse pounded at the sight of her, or how much her presence distracted him, he still was anxious to find out the truth.

Tara flipped through the pages. "I'm certain that all four letters were penned by my aunt, and they weren't sent through the mail. They were hand delivered by a private source. And as alluded to in her journal, Mr. Schlosser was one of my aunt's trusted contacts."

He scooted closer to her. "Do the letters talk about the gold?"

"Yes, and I think I've read enough of my aunt's journal to put most of it together. But it's not at all what I expected."

"Really?" Aaron tried to read her expression, but he couldn't. Disappointment? Loss? Relief?

He stared at the letters in her hands. They were the last link he had to the gold, and if they didn't come through with a new lead, he was heading back to Washington to report to his superiors. His last trip back to the capitol if things went his way today.

She handed him the first page from the short stack of communication. "In early 1865, Mr. Schlosser was fighting against the South in Virginia. One of the prisoners started bragging about his part in stealing a large amount of gold from the US Army. Whatever the man said apparently was enough to convince Mr. Schlosser that he was telling the truth about the stolen cache." She pointed to the bottom of the letter he held. "When my aunt found out about the gold from Mr. Schlosser, she believed that the money would aid the North in the war and decided to take it upon herself to find it."

"She must have been quite a woman. She was working for her country during a dangerous time." He scanned through the flowery-written letter before catching Tara's gaze. "So what happened to the gold?"

"Following Mr. Schlosser's information, she tracked the stolen cache to a farm outside Browning City, but when she got there it was too late."

"Too late? What do you mean?"

She offered him the second letter. "The details are scant at this point. All I can figure out is that someone got wind of the fact that she was looking for the gold. In any case, when she arrived at the farmhouse, three men, dressed in black, were in the process of removing the gold from the premises. She hid in a hayloft, then tried to follow, but ended up losing them. She wasn't ever able to pick up their trail again. She even told the local authorities, but they never came up with a solid lead to find the men, either. It was as if the gold vanished into thin air."

"Wow." Aaron slapped the letters against his leg.

Her lips curled into a solemn frown. "It's another dead end, Aaron."

This time, he didn't miss the disappointment in her eyes. He longed to reach out and hold her hands. To pull her into his arms and assure her that he didn't care if she was a spy, a farmhand, or the president of the United States, for that matter. To him, she was everything he'd ever dreamed of in a woman . . . in a wife.

But the timing wasn't right yet.

Instead, he gripped the armrests of the rocker instead. "Are you disappointed?"

"To be honest?" She looked up at him from beneath her long, dark lashes. "I don't think I care about the gold anymore."

"I thought you had your heart set on finding it."

"I did. At one time, anyway." She brushed a stray lock of hair away from her face. "In reading these letters, I had to wonder why my aunt never mentioned any of the details of her coming to Browning City and searching for the gold in her journal."

"Maybe she stopped writing for a while."

"Maybe, but what really surprised me was her last letter." She ran her hand across one of the worn pages, then outlined her aunt's signature with the tip of her finger. "She expressed feelings that her role as a courier wasn't making an impact in the outcome of the war. That was why she wanted to find the gold." Her eyes darkened. "I can't understand how she could ever feel that way. She was one of the heroes of the war in my eyes."

"She was a hero." Aaron searched for an answer that didn't sound pat. "Maybe, in her mind, she felt that passing information wasn't important enough, and she wanted to do something bigger."

Tara laughed, but he didn't miss the frustration behind the gesture. "If you're right, then what about me? I've spent my whole life trying to live up to her. And she didn't think that what she did was enough?"

He shook his head. "You don't have to pass messages behind enemy lines or find a missing cache of gold to be of value."

"I know." For the first time since his arrival, her face brightened into a smile. "The truth is, while I may not have found what I was after, I have found something far more priceless. I've finally been able to realize that I don't have to prove myself to be of value. I just need to serve God with my whole heart. Nothing more is required of me. Big or small, I just need to do it for Him."

Aaron let out a low whistle. "You're not the only one who needs to confess, then. I've lived my life seeking the wrong things. Did I ever tell you what my whole name is?"

Tara shook her head.

"Aaron Thomas Jefferson. My parents named me after one of their heroes, President Jefferson."

She arched her brow. "A big name to live up to."

"And in turn, I've spent every moment working to live up to my family's expectations. I've done the same things spiritually, as well, in trying to work for my salvation. It struck me when we talked about what Christ did on the cross that I don't have to do that. The cost has already been paid. I've spent far too long trying to show that I'm someone — something I never needed to do. Aren't we all already someone in God's eyes just being His creation made in His image?"

"You'd think that it would be an easy lesson to learn, wouldn't it?"

Aaron set the letters he held on the small table beside him and moved to stand by the porch railing. "There is another thing I've realized these past few days, as well."

Tara caught that same look in his eyes that made her heart stand still and the rest of her want to swoon. She rose to join him. "What is that?"

"I thought I should wait until we knew each other longer, but I'm not going to." He reached out to grasp her hands, then pulled them toward his chest. "I've realized that I don't want to spend the rest of my life without you, Tara. I want you to marry me."

"Marry you? I . . ." For a moment, she was lost in his gaze and couldn't speak. So much had changed since she'd left Boston. She'd believed that coming to Iowa would strengthen her worth. Instead, she'd found that the strength she'd longed to find was already within her — through Christ.

And now Aaron wanted to marry her!

He moved away from her. "I'm sorry. I have spoken too soon and out of turn. I know we haven't known each other long, but —"

"No. It's not that at all." She took a step forward into his arms. "Have you ever had a dream, and when it came true, you couldn't believe it was actually happening?"

He held her hands and rubbed the backs of her fingers with his thumbs. "I guess I've felt that way with you since the day we met. I had a hard time believing you were real."

"What do you mean?"

He lowered his face until she could feel his breath tickling her cheek. "I've spent my life waiting for God to send me someone who would make my life complete. Once I found you . . . well, it's sufficient to say that I don't ever want to lose you."

His kiss left her breathless. For once, something out of her dreams measured up in real life. After a lingering moment, he pulled away and ran his thumb down her cheek.

"You're beautiful."

"I never answered your question." She laughed as he matched her smile.

"Will you?"

"Yes. Of course I'll marry you." Her gaze swept across the picturesque landscape surrounding the farmhouse that had come to feel like home. "Does that mean I get to live in Iowa the rest of my life?"

"Not necessarily. I'll move to Boston if it means being with you."

She shook her head and wrapped her arms around his neck. "I might be a city girl, but if you have your heart set on a farm in Iowa, then I don't want to be any other place."

There was no denying the joy in his expression. "So you're becoming a country girl?"

She grabbed his hat from the post beside her and shoved it on top of her bonnet. "What do you think?"

"Now all you need is a pair of denim overalls." Laughing, he pulled down the brim until it covered her eyes. "I have to ask you one thing, or it's going to nag at me forever."

She pushed the hat back out of her face. "What's that?"

"Mrs. Meddler said she saw you wearing my Stetson one afternoon —"

"What?" Tara covered her mouth and giggled. "She actually saw me?"

"That's what she said, but you're always so impeccably dressed, I simply couldn't think of a reason for you to be walking down Main Street wearing my hat."

Tara eyed him from beneath the wide brim. "I must confess. In all the confusion during the shootout, I picked your hat up off the floor and, since I was crawling, I set it on my head for safekeeping. Then I completely forgot what I had done until I was greeted along the boardwalk with a few odd looks."

"I imagine you looked rather stunning. Like right now." Aaron hung the Stetson back on the post rail before bending over and brushing her lips gently with his. "What are your parents going to say about me?"

Tara felt her stomach tense, but she was determined not to worry about a reaction from them that had yet to take place. "They weren't happy about my excursion to Iowa, as they call it. My mother especially. She has a heart of gold but can be rather difficult at times. They believe I'm simply going through a phase and expect me to come running home to the ease of city life after a few weeks on the farm."

He pulled her toward him and nodded. "So now that I've managed to convince you to marry this besotted lawman, I'm going to have to try my hand at convincing your parents?"

"Exactly."

# SIXTEEN

"I simply won't allow you to marry him, Tara Rachel Young. There is nothing more to discuss." Tara's mother leaned forward in the walnut-framed settee that had recently been reupholstered and took a nibble of chocolate-dipped shortbread.

Tara sat across from her in the parlor of her parents' fashionable Boston residence and bit her lip. Somewhere in the Bible there was a verse on being slow to speak and slow to anger. If ever there had been a time to heed such advice, it was now.

She ran her hand across the polished armrest. She'd always loved the room with its ruby colored walls, fringed swag window coverings, and ornate furniture. But today even the whatnot cabinet that displayed her mother's china, daguerreotypes, and prized Staffordshire dogs and figurines seemed overdone and made her long for the simplicity of the farm.

She watched her mother calmly pour a cup of tea as if they were discussing this year's weather or what play was currently running at the Boston Theatre. Two topics about which Tara cared nothing at the moment. Smoothing down the fabric of her violet chambray gauze dress, she didn't miss the irony of how completely unfit the new gown would be on the farm. She was certain her mother had meant the gesture as a peace offering, but to Tara it had become a reminder of what she missed. Gathering the eggs in the morning while watching the sun make its daily appearance, making jam for the tenants' wives, or knitting on the front porch while chatting about what was happening in town. She missed the Carpenters, Sampson, Mrs. Meddler, and especially she missed Aaron.

"Have a cup of tea." Her mother waved her hand at the table laden not only with the hot drink, cream, and sugar, but a large assortment of sandwiches, cakes, and scones, as well.

Tara eyed the tempting array placed artistically on the doily-lined platter. "Father and Aaron haven't arrived yet."

Her heart trembled as she spoke Aaron's name. With Mrs. Meddler's oldest daughter agreeing to take over her employment at the

Carpenters', Tara had arrived home two weeks ago, believing that the only way to share the news of her engagement was in person. After setting a wedding date for late November, Aaron had promised to join her as soon as he completed his work for the government. Now all that was left to do was convince her parents, her mother in particular, that marrying Aaron was the right thing to do.

"They're late, and the tea is getting cold." Her mother reached out a pudgy hand and poured a second cup from the Chinese porcelain pot that had belonged to her great-grandmother. That one item was worth more than all the Carpenters' serving dishes put together.

Tara took the still-steamy drink that perched on the edge of the side table and managed a sip. Her mother believed in tea at four and wanted no excuses for tardiness. But there was more to today's bad-temperedness than simply a delayed guest. Her mother's testy moods were getting more and more difficult to handle, and Tara knew the source to be her unexpected engagement to a man her parents had never met.

Tara breathed in the orange fragrance of the tea and frowned. "So that's it? Subject closed?"

Her mother added a scone topped with Devonshire cream to her plate. "You can't be serious about marrying a man from Iowa of all places —"

"He's not from Iowa." Tara leaned forward. "He's from Philadelphia, he works for the government, and —"

"— he wants to run a farm. I know." Her mother settled back into the sofa. "Tara, please. How many times do I have to tell you that the idea is absolutely ridiculous? It's one thing to be a guest on a farm for a few weeks and perhaps help with some of the simple tasks, but running a farm is an entirely different matter."

Tara set down her teacup, afraid she might throw it across the room. She was tired of all the questions and nagging she'd endured since her return home. She needed her mother to understand that she had fallen in love with Aaron Jefferson, and such a sentiment was not a passing phase.

She glanced at the carved clock that hung on the wall. Her father and Aaron were thirty minutes late. Tardiness was an intolerable offense to her mother, despite the fact that one had little control over trains and other public sources of transportation. Still, Tara needed Aaron to arrive before things progressed from a one-sided battle of words to something more lethal where she said something she'd regret.

Determined to keep her mouth shut, she took a bite of a cucumber basil sandwich. The savory hors d'oeuvre the cook made used to be her favorite, but today the dainty snack tasted as dry as a pile of hay. No doubt her father was giving Aaron a similar lecture right now on why his daughter, who had been educated to live among Boston's society, would never adjust to life on a farm.

How to prove her parents were wrong was the question.

Tara couldn't help but try again. "Mother, all I ask is that before you pass judgment on someone you've never met, please just wait until you meet Aaron. I don't want to argue with you, but I came to love Iowa. And it's true that farming is not for everyone, but it's for us. For Aaron and me."

Her mother patted the back of her coiffed hair that had been tastefully dyed to cover the gray she would never admit existed. "I raised you to marry someone in a position of influence and authority. This trip to Iowa was supposed to be a short stint to show you a bit of the world and prepare you to settle down." Her mother's teacup clanked inside the saucer as she placed it on the side table. Her eyes, rimmed in black kohl, widened in anger. "But instead you agreed to marry, without our permission, the first ruffian who shows the least bit of interest in you."

Tara scrunched up her cloth napkin between her fingers. It was no use. She would never convince her mother that marrying Aaron was what was best for her life. She'd have to wait until he arrived and pray that he could somehow charm his way into her mother's heart the same way he'd won her over.

The door in the front hall opened, and Tara felt her stomach clench. She had no plans to disrespect her parents, but she was nineteen and certainly old enough to make her own decisions. Why, she was practically an old maid!

A moment later, Aaron stood in the doorway. It had seemed like forever since she'd seen him, but his presence in the room only made her more certain of her decision.

His eyes brightened at the sight of her, and he offered her a broad smile. "Tara. It's so good to see you —"

"You all are late." Her mother stood and pushed her skirts behind her. "Come and sit down before your tea turns stone cold."

Her father set his hat on the back of a

chair. "Darling, I want to first introduce you to Mr. Aaron Jefferson from Philadelphia."

Tara rose slowly to stand beside her mother, wishing she could have a moment alone with Aaron before facing her parents. His face was freshly shaved and as handsome as ever. Black hair lay curled against his collar, and his white shirt showed off his tanned skin. After a moment, she managed to tear her gaze from Aaron to look at her father who was smiling as he rubbed the edges of his mustache. Her gaze went back to Aaron. He was smiling, as well. Something had obviously transpired between the two men on the route from the train station to the house.

Aaron stepped up to greet her mother. "Mrs. Young. I'm pleased to finally make your acquaintance."

"Likewise, Mr. Jefferson." Her mother's frown had yet to vanish. "I've heard so many things about you."

"All good, I hope." Aaron laughed. "And I must say, if I didn't know better, I would have thought the two of you were sisters, Mrs. Young."

From her mother's expression, Aaron's words did little to ease the tension in the room.

Her mother sat back down. "Flattery and

smooth talk should be left at the door, Mr. Jefferson. Neither are welcome in this house."

"Mother." Tara's eyes widened as the four of them sat down in silence. The rhythmic ticking of the clock became the only sound piercing the heavy mood that circulated though the room.

Aaron stole a glance at Tara perched beside him on the edge of the sofa. Her expression had paled at her mother's comment, but he didn't miss the determination in her eyes. Somehow, he'd forgotten how beautiful she was. Her hair was swept up under a new hat with purple flowers on top and velvet ribbons hanging down the back. Her matching dress was just as stunning. But that's not what he had missed. He'd missed her laugh, her conversation, and the way she always managed to make him smile. He longed for a moment of privacy to take her into his arms and tell her how much he loved her.

With her mother's piercing gaze fixed on him, he instead studied the painted wall that was covered with framed floral drawings and struggled with how best to approach the woman. While Mr. Young had seemed agreeable with the proposed wedding, he had told

Aaron quite plainly that he was going to have to find a way to charm his wife if she was ever to agree to the marriage. The older man had given him two hints. Flowers and politics.

Aaron cleared his throat and managed a smile. "I understand you have a passion for gardening, Mrs. Young."

"I do, in fact." Mrs. Young's words were clipped as she stirred her tea. "Azaleas, roses, violets, morning glories, orchids . . ."

Aaron clasped his hands together in front of him and leaned forward. "I don't think I ever mentioned this to Tara, but my uncle was an orchid hunter. He was sent to South America to find a particular rare species for a wealthy Englishman."

Mrs. Young quirked an eyebrow. "Really?"

"Yes, and let me tell you, such a job was not for the faint of heart." He waved his arms in an exaggerated gesture. "When my uncle was twenty years old, the demand by the wealthy for orchids had grown to such frenzy that it was necessary for those wishing to acquire different varieties of the rare flower to send well-chosen gardeners and other such qualified men on a remote quest to find them. To many, money was no object, so they offered a huge reward to those who would risk their lives in search of a new breed of orchid."

He allowed the intensity in his voice to grow. "Their travels took them around the world to places like the Far East and South America, and through it all they had to deal with the ever-present dangers of disease, venomous snakes, wild animals, and savages."

"Savages?" Mrs. Young jumped back.

"Oh yes, and the competition was fierce. These men were often corrupt and had no qualms about stooping to spying, an assortment of unlawful activities . . . and even murder."

Tara stifled a giggle beside him, while Mrs. Young sat speechless. Even Mr. Young seemed intrigued by the tale.

"Whoever managed to survive these perils," Aaron continued, "and bring the plants back safely to Europe were bestowed with riches, and at times the orchids were even named for the one who found them."

"I've always had an interest in growing things." Tara's mother didn't try to hide the excitement on her face. "And the orchids. I've seen a few rare samples myself. They have such breathtaking colors."

"I, too, have an interest in horticulture." Aaron picked up a bite-sized crab puff off his plate and popped it into his mouth.

"You do?"

He nodded and swallowed. "I know Tara has told you about our plans."

"She spoke of farming." The smile on Mrs. Young's face disappeared. "I must say quite honestly, Mr. Jefferson, that a farm in Iowa is not what I had in mind for my only daughter."

Aaron sampled a slice of cake next, forcing himself to stay calm and focused. "Have you ever been to Iowa, Mrs. Young?"

The woman's expression hardened. "No."

"This is delicious, by the way." He held up the marbled sweet. "Imagine this, if you will. While the country might not have all the conveniences of the city, one awakes each morning to a sunrise unlike anything you've ever seen before. And that's just the beginning. Quiet prairies, dotted by wildflowers, stretch on mile after mile. The soil is fertile enough to grow an ear of corn twice the size of my hand."

"Really?" Mrs. Young glanced at her husband. "What kind of farm are you proposing?"

"We have many different options, really. Cattle, horses, pigs, and of course, corn, to name a few."

"From what I've gathered, Mr. Jefferson is quite a lawman." Mr. Young spoke up for

233

the first time since their arrival. "Worked on government cases in Washington until more recently when he was commissioned to work an important field assignment for them. And there's one other fact that might interest you, darling. Did Tara ever mention to you that Mr. Jefferson is related to former President Thomas Jefferson?"

"President Jefferson." Mrs. Young set down her teacup and pressed her hand against her chest. "Why, I do believe you have a bit of political blood running through your veins, then, after all."

The smile on Mrs. Young's face was subtle, but he didn't miss it. She rose from her chair and strode to the bookshelf located on the far side of the room. "I just happen to have a book on the man in my collection, and to think that you're related to him."

While Mrs. Young searched the bookshelf, Tara turned to Aaron. "You never told me you were related to President Jefferson."

"You never asked." He reached out and boldly squeezed her hand. "I didn't think that fact would matter to you."

"It doesn't, but . . ."

He leaned forward to whisper. "Your father told me that we were going to have to pull out every trump card I had to offer."

Mr. Young cleared his throat. "I think

there's really only one question left to ask the young man, darling."

Mrs. Young turned with the book in her hand. "And what would that be?"

Mr. Young caught his gaze. "Mr. Jefferson, do you love my daughter?"

There was no doubt in Aaron's mind. "Yes, sir, I do. And I'm willing to spend the rest of my life making her happy."

"Tara, why didn't you tell me that your Mr. Jefferson was such a charming man? I'm pleasantly surprised." Mrs. Young waltzed back across the room. "And Mr. Jefferson, I do hope you're planning to stay for dinner so we will have a chance to further discuss your . . . and my daughter's plans for the future. November, you said?"

Tara nodded.

"Then there's no time to lose. We have a wedding to plan."

# EPILOGUE

*Two months later*

Tara stood in front of the full-length beveled mirror, admiring the exquisite pattern of her wedding dress. Rays of morning sunlight broke through the stained glass window in the small room of the church, catching the silvery glint of the hand-sewn sequins that ornately lined the edges of the silky material. Following the style set three decades earlier by Queen Victoria's marriage, the white dress was a work of art. There was one thing she couldn't argue with. Her mother's tastes were impeccable.

From the moment Aaron first spoke of his uncle's adventures as an orchid hunter and his being related to President Jefferson, he'd managed to work his way straight into her mother's world. It had been nothing short of a miracle in Tara's eyes. Not that the planning of their wedding had been completely void of arguments, but Tara had learned early on that the best way for them all to get along was simply to let her mother work out the majority of the details. Whether lavender ham tea sandwiches or sage cheese wafers were served after the ceremony or which flowers adorned the bridal bouquet mattered little to her. All that she really cared about was the fact that she was about to become Mrs. Aaron Thomas Jefferson.

Even now, with the ceremony in less than thirty minutes, her mother had run off to discuss some grave concern with the minister. Tara wasn't even sure what the issue was. She pinched her cheeks to add a touch of extra color to her complexion. Aaron had been right when suggesting they should have eloped, but they both realized that such an act would have robbed her parents of the joy of seeing their only daughter marry. And that was something Tara was unwilling to do, as much as the idea of the two of them escaping the frenzy of the wedding appealed to her. In any case, she and Aaron planned to board a train for Iowa where they would begin their life together this very day.

A sharp knock on the door drew her out of her reverie.

"Mother?" She opened the door partway, then sucked in a deep breath. "Aaron?"

"Hi."

Her breathing quickened at the sight of him. "What are you doing here? Tradition forbids you to see me until the ceremony —"

"You look beautiful."

Tara felt a blush creep up her cheeks, and her knees threatened to give way beneath her. She regarded his colorful attire and his freshly shaved face, and she breathed in the fresh scent of his shaving soap. His mulberry frock coat and gray trousers made him look far more dashing than any other gentleman she'd ever seen.

Who really cared about tradition, anyway?

He leaned against the doorframe, his gaze never leaving her face. "Between formal teas in your honor and a constant array of wedding plans, I've missed you."

She was certain he'd still be able to make her blush fifty years from now. "We'll be married within the hour —"

"After which I must endure the five-course meal your mother planned, along with hours of socializing and other such formalities." He shot her a lopsided grin before leaning forward and brushing his lips across hers. "I just needed five minutes with you. Alone."

His words brought a smile to her lips. "We

should have eloped."

He eyed the empty hallway. "There's still time. We could be on the next train to Iowa . . ."

"My mother would send a pack of lawmen after us."

"I know." He laughed as he took her hand and rubbed her fingers. "I promise I'll leave, but I've been thinking about something."

"What's that?"

"The missing gold might have only have been a rumor, but —"

"Someone will find the gold one day." She flashed him a smile. "I'm certain of that."

"Maybe, but I think there's one thing we can both agree on."

"And what is that?"

He leaned down for a second kiss. "The gold doesn't matter anymore, because I've found something far better than any hidden treasure. I love you, Tara soon-to-be Mrs. Jefferson."

She reached up to kiss him back. "And I love you, Mr. Jefferson."

Tara stepped into his warm embrace and sent up a prayer of thanks. They'd both found treasure — not only in the rewards of their spiritual journey but also in each other. And that, in itself, was worth far more than any riches of this world.

# ABOUT THE AUTHOR

**Lisa Harris** and her husband, Scott, along with their three children, live in northern South Africa, where they work as missionaries. When she's not spending time with her family, her ministry, or writing, she enjoys traveling, learning how to cook different ethnic foods, and going on game drives through the African bush with her husband and kids. Find more about her latest books at www.lisaharriswrites.com